Blood and Moonlight

Legacy of Embers

By Olyn Moon

STHENOTYPE

Cover art by Laura Farley
Editing by Michael Allen

First Edition 2024

ISBN 979-8-9873772-6-0

Published by SthenoType
Medford, NJ 08055
www.SthenoType.com

For Laura Farley, who, without her help,
this book would not be what it is today.
She made me keep at it and turn it from
half a story to what it became.
And also provided me with an amazing cover.

Chapter One

My name is Rai Eckles, pronounced 'Ray' thanks to my eccentric parents, who are still the weirdest part of my life. Which is saying something, considering the disastrous year I've had. Last spring, my life changed in ways that I could never have imagined, and like most tales, it all began on an ordinary day. My best friend since childhood, Ashlan Ulfr, had also been accepted to the same small-town college in southern California. He was mainly there for the surfing, as the dorms were just a short walk from the beach. Ash had been chasing waves since our middle school days. Now in our third year of college, he still insisted on dragging me out of bed before dawn to catch the sunrise at the beach. While he surfed with ease and grace, I would sit back and watch the sun ascend over the water's horizon. Despite my lack of skill on a board, I cherished these early morning moments with him. Despite numerous attempts on his part, I could never quite grasp the art of surfing. On that day, everything felt perfect as I sat on the beach and watched the sun cast its warm glow across the horizon. Rays of light chased away the darkness, and it brought with it a sense of peace and tranquility. Little did I know that this feeling wouldn't last forever. Lost in the beauty of our surroundings, I barely registered when Ash approached me.

The sunlight danced over his tanned and glistening body as he towered over me. He pushed his short red hair back from his eyes, and flashed me his signature smile, complete with one dimple that never failed to charm anyone

1

who saw it. That combined with ocean-blue eyes that shone like gemstones, Ash was hard not to admire. It took some effort on my part to break my gaze from his chiseled abs and focus on what he was saying.

"Are you sure you don't want to come out and join me, Rai?" he asked, unaware of my gawking.

He pronounced my name like 'Rye,' a nickname he had given me when we were four years old. It was a name that only he could call me without me protesting.

"Water and boards never mix well for me, you know that," I replied with a chuckle.

"Yeah, yeah, but we turn twenty-one today," Ash said with a laugh as he dried himself off with a towel. "Maybe your luck has changed with age."

I couldn't help but smile at his optimism. Oh right, I almost forgot to mention. We shared the same birthday, down to almost the exact minute. Just another oddity in my life. How many people can say they've celebrated sixteen birthdays with the same person? We stayed at the beach for another hour before Ash had to head to class. That left me with enough time for a short nap before my own classes.

It was a weekend, and, as expected, Ash had big plans for our milestone birthday. Bar hopping was on the agenda, now legally, of course. It took copious amounts of caffeine to keep me awake during my final class of the day, English Lit, at seven p.m. Once it was over, I headed back to our shared apartment and got ready for the night ahead. To my surprise, Ash wasn't home yet. By the time I finished my shower thirty minutes later, I was greeted by the loud cacophony of voices coming from the living area.

"We're going to finally get you laid!" exclaimed Greg, one of Ash's friends from our first year of college.

I rolled my eyes and made my way past them to my room in just a towel.

"Let's get ready to burn this town down," James added with a beer can in hand.

He was a new addition to Ash's ever-growing group of friends, a member of the surf team that had been trying to recruit Ash. As I walked by, I could see Ash smiling at them, but his eyes betrayed his true feelings. He mouthed an apology to me, and I shrugged it off with a smile. But from the look on his face, I knew he saw through my facade as easily as I saw through his. His tight black tank top accentuated his sculpted body, and his fitted blue jeans showed off his best assets. I couldn't help but notice the custom Nike's on his feet, a gift I had given him five years ago featuring intricate ocean wave designs. In contrast, I wore something simple and comfortable, topped with a black beanie that Ash had gifted me two years prior. By the time I was ready, the group was eager to head out and barely spared me a glance as they ushered Ash out of the building.

Ash had always been popular, even back in grade school. And while we had been close friends since childhood, I struggled to make any other connections. College hadn't changed that dynamic at all. Despite my efforts, it seemed like I was invisible next to Ash, who effortlessly drew people towards him. I followed behind the crowd like a shadow, feeling insignificant compared to them. Having not been to any of the parties Ash had attended growing up, I was not much of a drinker. So, the first few stops I sipped on Jack and Coke, light on the Jack. Even the rowdy frat boys were taking it easy at this early hour, but around midnight, when we arrived at our fourth stop for the night, I overheard them discussing an underground bar that had just opened. The way they talked about it made it sound like it had everything anyone could ever want. With the way they said everything, they meant everything. I shook my head in disbelief and went to the restroom. When I returned, they were nowhere to be seen. Panic started to rise in my chest as I searched the crowded bar for any sign of Ash or the others. I couldn't believe it! They had left me…

"What the…" I muttered to myself.

I couldn't believe he would just leave me on our birthday so easily. Feeling hurt and abandoned, I turned around and almost collided with a short pale woman who seemed around my age. Though it was hard to tell with the long black hair that covered most of her face, except one dull green eye.

"Oh! I'm so sorry," I apologized reflexively.

She glared at me with her one visible eye for a moment, before her expression lightened.

"No, no. It was my fault. I should pay more attention to where I'm going," she replied politely.

"No, it's fine," I said as I scanned the crowd in search of my friend.

"Missing someone?" she asked sympathetically.

"Just trying to find my friend."

"What do they look like? Maybe I can help," she offered.

"Unnaturally tall, red hair, tan, life of the crowd," I said with a shrug, "You know the normal types that manage to get lost."

"Tan, and red hair? Doesn't sound normal to me. But if it is the same person, I think I saw him leave with a group of people a few minutes ago."

The shock must have been evident on my face

because she put a hand on my shoulder. Even through my shirt, her hands felt like ice, and I shuddered involuntarily.

"It's a bit cold in here," I said quickly as she pulled her hand away.

"Believe it or not, my friends also ditched me. I think I saw them mixed in with the crowd your friend left in. By the time I could push through the crowd, they were gone, and I couldn't tell which way they all went," she said almost too softly for me to hear.

"You wouldn't know about some underground club, would you?"

"I heard my friends talking about going. But not one of them bothered to tell me where to go. I feel like I'm just invisible at times," she sighed.

"Believe me I know that feeling. Especially next to my friend, people tend to look right past..." My words trailed off as I realized we had made our way outside. Confusion crossed my face as I looked around, the warmth of the night soothing me. "How?"

"Oh, sorry. I needed some fresh air, and you just followed along as I moved," she said with a small smile. "My name's, Theresa Wentzel, by the way. Most just call me, Tessa, though."

"Um, Rai Eckles," I replied with an awkward little wave.

As Tessa produced a small USB-like vape from her pocket, I noticed a glint of gold on her lip. The vapor she exhaled enveloped us in a sweet, fruity scent.

"Do you live near?" I asked as I tried to make conversation.

"Sorta. Just moved here today actually. Most places are just temporary, my family moves around a lot. But maybe

5

this time will be different."

"Well, since we've both been abandoned, want to go see a great late-night diner?" I mumbled, I thought too quietly.

"Sure!" she said enthusiastically, "Do they have milkshakes?"

"Of course. That's the main reason I go," I said with a grin and walked away.

I didn't hear her footsteps follow and cursed to myself. Of course, she won't go with some stranger at nearly one in the morning. I turned around and she was nowhere in sight.

"Leave something?" Tessa's voice came from the left of me.

"N, no. Sorry. Let's go."

A few blocks away stood an old-fashioned diner straight out of a 1950's movie. The red and white checkered motif adorned the exterior, and women with beehive hairdos scurried about inside. The only difference was that these women were middle-aged instead of teenagers. The circular booths were lined with surprisingly comfortable red leather seats. As we slid into one booth on opposite sides, our waitress approached us, smelling of cigarette smoke and mint.

"What can I get y'all?" the waitress drawled in a bad, exaggerated southern accent.

"Plate of cheese fries and a chocolate shake for me," I answered, then looked at Tessa, "What would you like?"

"Just a vanilla shake," whispered Tessa.

"Alrighty, it'll be right out," the waitress said and walked away.

As we waited for our food, there was an awkward silence between us. I tried to start a conversation, but I've always been terrible at talking. The only person I could really talk to was Ash, but he usually did most of the talking, so there was never any awkwardness between us. It felt like an eternity waiting for our order, as we both stared down at the table.

"Here y'all go," the waitress announced, breaking the silence.

I looked up as she placed down the order along with two straws, then left. Tessa slid hers over without looking up.

"Tastes good," Tessa said as she still looked down.

"Yep. It's a great spot for cramming sessions. I'm in here a lot during finals."

She looked up at me.

"College, not high school," I said quickly.

She chuckled, "I never went. My…uncle, he saw it as a waste of time."

"What about your parents?"

"They stopped being around in my last year of high school," she answered cryptically.

"Oh," was all I could mutter, "So, then what brings you down to SoCal?"

"My uncle travels a lot. For business," she added quickly. "I live with him, and he always sells the house when we move to the next town. So, I follow him and my other family."

"Must be lonely."

"You can be somewhere forever and still be lonely."

"That is true. Unless you're lucky. Speaking of…I know a good spot for breakfast if you are ever in the mood."

She looked down, but I swear I saw her blushing as she did.

"I'm not really a morning person…but I wouldn't

mind meeting here again some other night," she said softly, without looking up.

I borrowed a pen from the waitress as I paid the bill and wrote my number for her on a napkin. Then I walked her to the entrance of a gated community about a mile from my dorm.

"Well, this is me," she said, "I should be fine from here."

"Oh, wow. Your uncle's business seems good."

"Something like that. Thank you for staying with me. If you hadn't, I would have been stuck in that bar alone."

"You helped me too. It wasn't really my scene. But friends like dragging you to places to get out."

She smiled sadly and turned away.

"I'll call you soon," she said and made her way inside the gates.

I waved as she disappeared into the night and turned to walk home. It was nearing dawn by the time I made it back, but it seemed like Ash also hadn't made it back. The area where we kept our shoes was empty, and his door was standing wide open. I was too tired to care that it was closed when we left and was asleep almost instantly as I hit my bed, still fully clothed. The sun was hanging low in the sky by the time I woke up. Groggily, I brushed my teeth and washed my face before heading into the kitchen. Ash's door still stood open, and the bed was unslept in. I wasn't worried. He did it a lot, to be honest. Since we were teenagers, he would disappear for a few days every month. He never talked about why or where he went. It was the only secret he kept from me. He said it was just a family obligation. And even the distance we had put between us, and our hometown had not stopped it. I lost myself in making breakfast for dinner. Eggs, homemade waffles, and bacon. The sun set as I whisked away at the batter for my waffles, and my phone buzzed, interrupting my early aughts pop punk music.

Would you be up for anything tonight?

That was the message on my phone from an unknown number. As I stared at it, another message popped up.

Oh right. This is, Tessa. If you remember me, I'm not sure if you do.

I smiled to myself as I answered.

My roommate is probably out for the next few days. We can watch a movie or something. I'm making waffles if you want some.

I then sent my address and set about making more batter for the waffles. As I did, she responded she would be over soon. I was finishing the clean-up part of cooking when a small knock came at the door. It almost didn't register, it was so quiet. As it did, I rushed to the door, suddenly aware that I was in last night's clothes. When I opened the door, I stood in awe. She was standing there, her hands fidgeting in front of her. Her black sundress stood out in contrast to her pale skin. Her hair was up in a loose bun, and the bright red mascara around her emerald eyes made them even more captivating. Noticing the navy-blue lipstick made me realize I was standing there with my mouth hung open. I closed my mouth and stepped to the side to let her in. She hesitantly put

9

a foot forward, then set it back down.

"Sorry, I've been raised that it's impolite to enter somewhere when you haven't been invited in. It sounds so archaic saying that aloud," she cringed and looked down at the floor, "But, old habits and all that."

"Oh, uh, sorry. Come in," I said, "The couch is to the left, the kitchen is behind it. I need to clean up quickly. I tend to make myself a bit of a mess when I'm cooking. I will be right back and then we can eat."

I'm not exactly sure how much she understood in my jumble of quick mumbled words, but as she stepped inside, I was closing my bedroom door. I threw clothes around, trying to find something that wasn't wrinkled or dirty, since I hadn't done laundry that week. It took me longer than I wanted, but after a few minutes, and a quick brush of my hair, I was out. She sat on the edge of the couch, her back completely straight.

"Sorry that took so long," I mumbled.

"It's okay. The waffles smell delicious," she said with a small smile.

"They're amazing, trust me," I responded with a smile back, "Let me get plates."

After eating, we turned on a movie. After a ton of debate over which genre was the best in horror, we settled on watching Warm Bodies. Mainly because we decided on a zombie movie, and it was the only one in the house, thanks to Ash. She had thought Ginger Snaps was the best movie, as she was adamant that werewolf movies were the best genre. I was for an older movie called Frighteners, because I think ghost movies are the best, but a little comedy is needed.

"There was nothing scary about that movie," she pouted.

"I told you it was not going to be the standard zombie movie," I laughed.

"Who makes something like that?"

"Somebody who doesn't understand that Romeo and Juliet is a terrible love story."

Tessa looked at me and smiled, "Then we should watch The Craft next. Least it'll be horror this time."

"Fine, fine, you win, we will watch witches now," I said in a fake exasperated sigh.

Honestly, watching her enjoy the movie was much better than the movie, if I do say so myself. The movie itself was surprisingly good too, from what little I watched.

"You want to go get some ice cream? There's a great place down the block. But it does close in an hour," I said after the movie.

She jumped up and grabbed my hand. Despite the heat of the night, her hands were like ice. She saw me shiver and let go of my hand.

"Sorry. I forget my hands are always cold," she murmured.

"No, it's fine. Just unexpected," I said and took hold of her hand, "Let's go."

Her lips curved upwards in a soft smile as she intertwined her fingers with mine, and together we left the apartment. The Ice Cream Shoppe was a small, weathered hut nestled into a sprawling parking lot. Despite its size, it bustled with customers. As we neared the hut, I couldn't help but notice the delightful smells of freshly made waffle cones wafting through the air. After patiently waiting in line, we finally sat down on a nearby curb with our sweet treats in hand. Two swirled vanilla cones. With every lick and bite, I felt my heart flutter more for this girl by my side. As midnight

11

approached, I offered to walk her home. But to my surprise, she confidently declined and told me she would be fine before she took off in the opposite direction from my place. Left alone to contemplate the evening's events, I returned home and sank into my couch, unable to sleep as thoughts of her danced through my mind.

Chapter Two

I woke up to Ash shaking me awake.

"Did you fall asleep on the couch on purpose?" he asked when I opened my eyes.

He wore a towel around his waist, and another was draped over his head and shoulders. Steam rolled off his wet, golden, glistening torso from one of his scalding showers.

"Um," was all I could manage to say.

"Such a way with words," he joked, "Are you okay?"

"What? Oh, yeah, fine," I said as I sat up and looked away, "I must have fell asleep watching a movie."

"Ginger Snaps? A Werewolf movie? It's not even close to Halloween."

"I was in the mood. A new friend I met, when you decided to ditch me the other night, wanted to watch horror movies," I said groggily.

"Sorry man. By the time I realized what had happened, it was too late. Wait? Did you say new friend? Did you meet someone at the bar? Who are they? When do I get to meet them?" Ash asked excitedly.

"A woman named Tessa. We were both abandoned in the bar. I ran into her, literally. We bonded over that," I explained. "Those people you left with were her group."

"Oh. You're grown, so I don't want to tell you what to do, but those guys were not great," said Ash, "We ditched them almost instantly. We hadn't even known they were with us at first."

13

"Oh. Anyway, how was that place?"

"I didn't get to stay long. You know me, familia obligations are always most important no matter the time of day or night. I just got back in town this morning."

"I'm glad you're back before school this time. It's usually so much longer."

"It gets easier the older you are. Less of a pain. Anyway, when do I meet her?"

"I don't know, I just woke up. Let me eat first."

I pulled out a large slender cup, filled it with frosted flakes, then milk. You know, the right way to make cereal. When I finished, Ash was coming out of his room in camo cargo shorts and a black tank. I looked at my phone to see no new texts from Tessa. I hoped she had made it home safe.

"Why the pensive look?" Ash asked as he sat at the kitchen table holding a bagel.

"Huh?"

"You're staring at your phone and looking worried."

"Oh. She hasn't texted me back since last night. I was just thinking the worst," I muttered. "Who lets someone walk home alone?"

"Look at it this way, if you went all the way to her place, then you would have been the one walking home alone."

"I guess. Her place seemed safe looking."

"You've been to her house?"

"Sorta. I walked her to the gates of a community."

He stared at me for a moment, then shrugged.

"Any big plans? I haven't been out on the waves since our birthday, so if you want to come with me, it's where I plan to spend the rest of my day."

"Did you not just shower?"

14

"And you're welcome. If you had been awake when I came in, you'd have passed out. I was caked in dirt and sweat. I was not going to head down to the beach looking or smelling like that."

"Fair. Well, I have no plans, so I'll come."

"Are you going to get in?"

"No, just to hang out. The normal."

I dressed in a pair of shorts and a short-sleeve shirt before I followed Ash to the beach. I kept staring at my phone, disappointed when I had no messages. The afternoon was a slow blur. Ash surfed, I picked a shadowy rock outing to sit under, then we went to a boardwalk to get some funnel cake as the sun set. A normal weekend for us. We got home as the moon rose high into the sky. As I walked into the apartment, my phone buzzed. Ash laughed at me as I fumbled it out of my pocket, nearly dropping it as I did.

"Uhm, hey, Ash? What did you say happened to the people you left with?" I asked solemnly.

"I didn't. I have no idea. We ditched them at the club," replied Ash, "What's up?"

"Apparently they've not made it home yet," I answered and held up my cell.

He read Tessa's message, his features unreadable.

Sorry that I haven't been able to respond sooner.

My uncle has been worried about our family.

They still haven't returned since the other night.

Which isn't that unusual, but they haven't called either

"Well, I've got no clue what happened. Like I said, they were some bad people. They're probably in jail somewhere with all the things they could have gotten in that club," Ash said with a shrug.

Chapter Three

It was weeks before I heard from Tessa again after that. I had almost forgotten to think about her over the weekend when my phone buzzed one night as the sun set. I was cooking dinner and just assumed it was Ash, and didn't even think to check it, since I was in the zone while cooking. As the sauce for spaghetti simmered, I saw the green light flashing, checked what Ash wanted, and smiled down at my phone when I saw the name. The first message asked if I was busy. An hour later, there was a second message that I had not even realized had come through that said she was sorry for bothering me and understood. That had been an hour ago. I immediately texted her and apologized for not answering. I then sent a second and explained what had happened.

I waited patiently for her response as I finished my sauce and the noodles. It seemed like an eternity as I waited, but it was less than five minutes before she responded back. She sent a laughing face, and that she was glad I still remembered her. Then asked if I wanted to go out for shakes the next night. I asked her if she wanted to have dinner tonight at my place. After a long wait, she said she didn't want to impose, and I told her it would be no imposition. I always made enough for leftovers. Ash's friends liked to show up without any notice and ate a lot, just like Ash. For once, it was my turn to have someone show up unannounced, sorta. Ash came out of his room in just sweatpants as I set the table for

17

three. I hadn't even realized he had come back home while I was cooking.

"What's up?" Ash asked as he eyed the table, then looked around, "Did one of the guys show up? Did you ask them what happened to the other group?"

"No, and no. My friend is coming over. Guess you get to meet her finally. Please have a shirt on when she gets here."

He grunted and went back to his room as a knock came at the front door.

"Be right there!" I yelled as I took the last dish to the table.

When I opened the door, Tessa stood there in black cut up jeans, a worn Metallica shirt, and her hair was in a ponytail with her bangs framing her face.

"You…uh…look nice," I stuttered.

"Thanks," she said softly, and lowered her eyes down.

I stepped back and she came in as Ash came out from his room in a baggy maroon sweatshirt. I looked at him and thought I saw fear run across his face, but it was gone almost as quickly, if it had been there at all. I looked back to Tessa, and she had stiffened in the doorway.

"Oh, uh…sorry. I guess I didn't mention that Ash was here," I said quickly.

"Don't apologize," she said as she finished walking inside.

There was a palpable tension in the air as we ate. After he was done, Ash left, saying he had forgotten he needed to help a friend. As the door closed, I saw the tension leave Tessa's body.

"Are you okay?" I asked concerned.

"I'm fine," she said with a half-smile, "My uncle would love your cooking. Would you mind doing it one day?"

"How big is the household?"

"Well, since my cousins left, it's just three of us usually. Me, my aunt, and my uncle. Plus a maid and butler that live in, so they are there all the time. Without the four other people, it is generally much too quiet though."

"They could come here," I offered.

"No! I mean no offense, sorry. They're just rich and uptight. They'd never be caught dead here. But if you're not busy, maybe you can come over to my place next weekend. They'd love to meet you."

"Uh, sure."

I was just falling asleep after walking Tessa to the gates of her community when the front door slamming jolted me awake. Ash was dripping with sweat as he walked by when I opened my door.

"What happened?" I asked.

When he didn't answer, I asked even louder. He ripped around towards me. His eyes were bright yellow and full of rage. I blinked and took a step back. When I opened my eyes, he looked at me worried, his eyes the normal bright blue.

"What's wrong? Did you say anything?" he asked.

"I was asking what happened. You're drenched," I answered as I wiped my eyes.

"Just got back from running. Had some steam to let out. This huge group project is due by the end of the week, and it's being difficult," sighed Ash.

"Good luck," I said and went back to bed.

The next few days felt so long. I couldn't sleep, and because of that I couldn't concentrate in my classes. Nightmares weren't a new thing, I mean everyone has them, but they came to me every time I closed my eyes. There were vague shapes in the darkness that chased me down. Sometimes on all fours, sometimes standing upright. No matter which way they chased me, whether they were huge and hulking canines or small and lithe humanoid, the shapes would catch me. Always catching me. Then there would be blood everywhere. My blood. I would shoot awake, covered in a cold sweat, as my last breath escaped my body, and I was ripped apart.

As I burnt some pancakes and set off the smoke alarm, Ash came over and laid a large hand on my shoulder.

"Are you doing okay? You've seemed distracted lately," he said. "This isn't the first time you've burned something in the last few days."

I mumbled that I was fine, and nothing was wrong, but he just stared at me. I don't know why he didn't believe me. Was it the dark circles under my eyes? Maybe. Was it the mumbling? Could be. Was it the burning of food? Most definitely. And as I looked up into those dazzling blue eyes, I couldn't lie. So with a heavy sigh, I told him that sleep was a luxury I hadn't been able to have. I was so exhausted. No, I was beyond exhausted. His eyes grew wider as I told him of the nightmares I had been having.

"No class for you for today. You will stay home, and I will be back ASAP. My grandmother had a remedy for my night terrors that will work wonders for you too," said Ash.

Then just like that, I was alone with nothing but a severely burnt breakfast, and a blaring smoke alarm. After turning that off, I decided to take Ash's advice and went to the couch to watch a movie. I must have drifted off to sleep, because the next thing I knew I was being shaken awake by Ash and covered in the same cold sweat.

"What happened?" I asked groggily.

"I was gonna ask you that. I got to the doorway, and you just started screaming like you were being killed. I'll be surprised if the cops don't show up."

"I don't remember anything…"

"Don't worry, I got the stuff you need right here," Ash said as he held up a plastic bag.

"What's in that?"

"Stuff for wardings so you can finally get rest."

"Do you really believe in that stuff?" I asked dubiously.

"I've seen it work personally. I cannot explain it to you, but I do know it will work. Trust me."

"Fine," I sighed, "Besides, what do I really have to lose?"

"Exactly. Now go get washed up while I do what I need to do. Then you will sleep like a log."

As I finished my hot shower and returned to my room, Ash was hanging up small pouches on the four cardinal directions in the middle of my walls.

"Are you sure about this stuff?" I asked again.

"Look, it's to cleanse evil spirits, and keep them away while keeping your mind calm. It's not much different than using a hot bath to get rid of stress."

After they were hung up, he lit each one, one by one, then put the flame out in the same order. A mint smell began to permeate my room like a type of incense. Suddenly I felt more tired than I ever had, and Ash helped me into my bed as my eyes grew heavier. Next thing I knew, my alarm was going off the next morning, and I was in my pajamas. I felt fabulous. It was the best sleep I had gotten since… well years to be honest.

"Finally up I see," Ash said as I came out of my

room.

"Yeah. Thanks. I can't believe that it really worked."

"Told you so. Doubting me after all this time," scoffed Ash.

"Now I won't be a total mess when I go over and meet Tessa's family.

"What?" exclaimed Ash.

"Yea. Tomorrow night I'm cooking for them."

"Are you sure that's wise? You've basically just met her."

"What? It's been like a month. It's not like she's some crazy killer."

"How do you know?"

"Because I'm still alive, for one."

"She could be giving you a false since of security."

"You've watched way too many movies, my dude," I laughed.

"Rai, listen to me. You cannot go to their house. And you definitely cannot go alone."

"Why?" I asked as I lifted an eyebrow.

"She's a vampire…"

Chapter Four

Ash was not amused when I burst out laughing and fell back onto the couch. He frowned at me until I stopped laughing.

"You really believe that? You're not joking?" I asked confused.

"I don't just believe it. I know it to be true. I've met some before."

"Ash…what happened to her cousins that went off with you?"

For the first time in my life, I feared Ash. Scared that he may have done something I couldn't have imagined he was capable of minutes ago. He was the sanest person in my life. At least I thought so, but now I thought he may have hidden a crazy that I never knew about. Was he really that one that everyone liked, but was really a serial killer? I mean, who believes in vampires?

"I don't know. I'm just trying to save you from those…creatures," Ash said exasperated.

"She's human man! What are you doing? Trying to freak me out? Cause it's working man. But of you not her," I exclaimed as I stood up.

A low growl escaped from his chest, and his eyes flashed yellow. I fell back onto the couch, and he stormed out. I had never seen him so angry since we started junior high, and it scared me.

He didn't come back that night, and he still wasn't

23

there when I woke up. I tried to put the altercation out of my mind and went to do my morning shopping. I hadn't had time to think about what I wanted to make Tessa's family, and I was hoping seeing the ingredients would spark inspiration. I started my afternoon with prepping a pot roast. The sun was setting when she answered my text of what time I should show up. About an hour later, she was at my door. Through all that time, Ash still hadn't returned, and I was worried about what he might have gotten into.

"Hello," she said as I opened the door.

"You didn't have to cook here," she said as she helped me gather the pots to bring.

"It takes time to prepare, and I wanted everything to be perfect. It's my first-time meeting someone, and I'll be nervous enough as it is, without trying to use new equipment that may be a lot more fancy than I know how to use," I explained.

Downstairs there was a long, black limousine.

"What is this?" I asked, stunned.

"You cannot walk that far with all this food. Besides, it was the least my uncle could do when you offered to cook," said Tessa.

A seven-foot-tall pale man in a black suit and tie opened the limo door. He was bald, wore dark sunglasses even though it was night, and there was a weird texture to his ears that I couldn't quite explain or understand.

"Thank you, Jeffery," Tessa said as she got into the limo.

"Thanks," I murmured as I got in behind her.

I'm not sure what I expected of the house, but what I saw was not it. The house was situated at the back of the community and took up its own block. A wooden fence enclosed the property, with a ten-foot-long metal gate as the only entrance up the driveway. The drive to the house was only a minute or two, but it was up a canopy tunnel of trees. For a moment, I felt I was in a secluded forest home. The streetlights behind us were all that shattered the illusion. The front door was twice my height and width. As we came up to the door, an old man opened it for us. He was stooped over, making him seem even smaller than he was, and he had large liver spots that dotted his hand as he ushered me in.

"I'll take him to the kitchen, Rafael. Tell my uncle that we are here," said Tessa.

"Yes madam," breathed Rafael.

He walked down the hall to the left, while I followed Tessa straight. The kitchen could have fit my whole apartment into it and still had room. It was closed off to the rest of the house, except for the one door we entered through. Everything was stainless steel and looked like a professional kitchen.

"This place is amazing," I gasped.

"My uncle likes to bring in famous chefs to cook, and they like to have everything available to them. We even hire staff that the chefs hand pick for the night when he does that," Tessa said with a wave of her hand.

Rafael came in and bowed as he said, "Your uncle wishes to see you, madam."

Tessa looked uneasily between me and Rafael.

"Stay here, I will be back as quickly as possible," she finally said.

A minute after she walked out, a very slim, but tall man walked in. He had short blonde hair and amber eyes. When he looked down at me and gave me a toothy smile, I couldn't suppress a shudder. He wore an immaculate gray suit with a red tie. His teeth were unnaturally white.

"My, my, my, who are you? You look delicious," he said in a falsetto voice.

"H...h...hi," I stuttered, "My n...nam...name is, Rai."

"And what brings such a snack as you to our kitchen?"

"Tessa," I blurted out.

"Oh? So, you are the special one."

There was a weird twinkle in his eyes as he spoke.

"Leave him alone, Jarret," Tessa said coldly from behind me.

I jumped at her voice and spun around.

"Oh, Little Tessa, I was just having a bit of fun," said Jarret innocently.

"Do it somewhere else. I didn't even know you were here," Tessa said in an almost growl.

He just smiled at her and sauntered away.

"Who...uh...who is that?" I asked.

"A very distant cousin. He's trouble, but he won't do anything as long as you are a guest to my, and his, uncle," said Tessa, "I'm so sorry about him. I didn't realize he had come."

"It's not your fault. Is he dangerous or something?"

"You'll be fine. He's like a cat. Mostly lazy and goes where he wants."

I raised an eyebrow at her.

"Forget him and follow me," she said and took my hand. The contact with her sent most thoughts from my head. She led me through a twisting hallway to stop in front of a large oak door. There was a face of a bat carved into it.

"Time to meet my aunt and uncle," said Tessa with a deep breath.

Chapter Five

She pulled open the door and put her hand out for me to go in first. Inside left me as awestruck as the kitchen. It was a giant library. Books adorned the walls around the space, and shelves ran parallel down the room. From what I could see they were also filled with books. My mouth must have been hanging open as I looked around, because a soft, cold hand touched my jaw, and I heard my teeth click together as I returned to my senses.

"This is the best place ever," I whispered.

"You have not even seen the best parts," giggled Tessa.

She led me through the aisles, all crammed with books. I wanted to explore and see how they were separated. There were old looking tomes on one aisle, then newer books down a different that we passed. In the middle of the room, through the maze of shelves, was a round, fluffy pillow couch that could have easily fit ten people relatively comfortable. Sitting on the opposite side of where we entered were two very young-looking people. They looked younger than I was. The man had a face full of freckles and dyed dark blue hair. He wore a wrinkled black suit with a red tie that hung loosely around his neck. The woman wore gray sweatpants and an oversized tie-dyed t-shirt. Her auburn hair was put into a loose bun, and she wore tiny, black-rimmed glasses.

They both closed their books and turned to smile at me. Large, toothy smiles that showed off sharp canines, that

27

didn't reach their eyes. Ash's words must have gotten to me, because I felt like a rabbit being stared down by a coyote. I shuddered and looked at my feet.

"Hi," I managed to mumble out.

"This is, Rai. Rai, this is my, Uncle Isiak, and Aunt Corri."

"So nice to meet you," said Corri, "We have heard so much about you."

Her voice was soft and silky.

"I cannot wait to taste what you have brought us," said Isiak.

His voice was deeper than I expected, with a slight accent that I couldn't place.

They stood up and he shook my hand. His hand was even colder than Tessa's if that was possible. Corri patted my shoulder, then offered me a seat.

"So, you're a student?" asked Isiak. "It seems forever ago since I went to college."

He must have seen the confusion on my face because he chuckled.

"I am older than I look. Great genes in my family, I suppose. I am almost twice Tessa's age," he said.

"Oh, Wow. I hope I still look so youthful when I'm older," I said.

"Only time will tell," chuckled Corri.

"Everyone should be here soon. Then we can eat," said Isiak.

There was a slight undertone to their words that made the hair on my neck stand up.

"Everyone?" Tessa and I asked simultaneously.

She sounded scared to my ears.

"The whole family is coming for dinner," Isiak said

28

with a smile.

"I don't think I have enough for more than five or six people," I stammered.

"No worries. They were all told to bring something themselves. Tessa has never brought one home, so I wanted the whole family to meet someone so special. The whole family is eager to meet the one our little Tessa talks about so often," said Isiak.

"Isiak," whimpered Tessa.

"No worries. It will all be fine," he said with a tone that said it was final.

"It's fine. Really," I said to her.

"We will see," she whispered.

"Go now. Get everything ready. We will be in the dining room soon. It was good to meet you, Rai," said Isiak.

"Yes, nice to meet you," said Corri.

"Nice to meet you both," I said.

Tessa was silent and kept her head down as we made it back to the kitchen. I was sad that we had left the library so quickly. It was just a treasure trove waiting to be explored. But, I would have plenty of time for that after dinner, I guessed.

"Are you okay?" I asked.

"Yes," she said curtly.

I grabbed her shoulder outside the kitchen and stopped her.

"You can talk to me you know. About anything."

"You will either understand soon, or it won't matter," she sighed.

She walked into the kitchen without waiting for a response. The food was already out and on serving trays that kept everything heated. I stood in the doorway, my mouth agape once again.

"You need to leave," Tessa said urgently.

"What?"

Before she could say anything else, Jarret came from the back area.

"Our servers took the liberty of preparing everything," smiled Jarret, "Are you two ready?"

"Sure. How many people are there?" I asked.

"Oh just a dozen or so," chirped Jarret.

"Is this Dolores' idea?" asked Tessa wearily.

"Grandmother had no part in this, I am afraid. It was all our great-great grandfather's idea. You know how protective he is of the family," beamed Jarret.

Tessa went rigid for a minute, then grabbed my hand so tightly I thought it was going to break. She mouthed sorry, and then led me towards the dining hall with Jarret in tow. She went to say something, but after a quick glance at Jarret, she stopped. The dining hall was as large as the kitchen, if not even more so. It had a high sloped ceiling, a row of crystal chandeliers, and I felt like I was in one of those royal feasting halls in a fantasy show. There was even a long table that ran the length of the room right in the middle of it. Seated on the closest end was Isiak, and on the opposite end was a considerably older gentleman. He had stark white hair and wrinkles. He looked like a skeleton wearing a meat suit without the muscles or organs.

"Oh, welcome," he bellowed as we walked in.

His voice seemed to fill the whole room. It was so boisterous and loud, the opposite of what my mind thought it would be.

"Good evening great-great grandfather," said Tessa with a curtsy.

"Come closer, it is so hard to see you both so far away. Is this the one you have spoken so highly of?" he said and gestured a long finger at me.

She nodded as we moved closer.

"Good evening," I said, my voice a bit shaky.

"This is, Yujin. He is the patriarch of my family. Great-great grandfather, this is my friend, Rai," said Tessa.

It seemed like his eyes bore into my soul as I looked straight into them. A faint hint of confusion passed quickly in those pale, yellow eyes of his, and he looked away. As I broke my gaze away, I noticed a dozen others staring at me in brief awe before looking away. All, that is, but Tessa.

"How?" she mouthed.

I cocked my head.

"What is going on and why is everyone down on your uncle's end?" I whispered.

"Yujin, has a terrible temper. Most of us try to avoid him or stay as far away as we can. But, he is going to want us to stay close to him," Tessa whispered back.

"I wish to retire," Yujin announced. "Carry on. I will see myself out."

He seemed to float to his feet and glide away with no other word. Tessa watched him leave with wide eyes. Everyone else was also in shock at his sudden departure.

"Guess he wasn't hungry," I joked.

"Curiouser and curiouser," Isiak said suddenly behind me.

Tessa grabbed my arm and jerked me behind her with an ease that should not have been possible.

"We're leaving also," she announced.

"No. You are not," Isiak growled.

Jarret and Corri had also come up, and I felt trapped

as I looked at each face on either side of us.

"You promised!" yelled Tessa.

"But they are so…fascinating. If they were to become one of us, there is no end to what they could do. We promised not to feed," said Isiak.

"Who? What's going on?" I asked.

"We want to make you one of us. Nobody can look Yujin in the eyes like that," said Isiak. "We were originally just playing with you to get at our little Tessa, but now we want you. Something about you turns off our view of you as a food source. You are so…intriguing in so many other ways though."

"Food? One of you? You can't be serious. I can't become a cannibal," I protested.

"Oh young one, we are not cannibals either," Corri interjected. "Well, I suppose our darker kin can be, but not us. We are of the night, not of the earth."

"We are vampir," said Jarret, Corri, and Isiak simultaneously.

Chapter Six

"Isiak!" boomed Yujin's voice from seemingly everywhere, "This young one is a guest in this house and shall be treated as one. And whence they leave, they shall be treated like family and off-limits to aggression from any of us."

All four around me flinched, and the three surrounding me took deep breaths as they backed away.

"We need to find you something new to eat," sighed Isiak.

I stared at everyone, too stunned to talk. Vampires weren't real. This had to be some weird hazing and wiring tricks. How did they get their eyes to turn blood red, though, or their already sharp canines to grow longer? That was not something I could explain. None of that was possible.

"Rai? Are you alright?" Tessa asked as she shook me lightly.

"I need to go," I said, "I don't know what sick game is going on here, but I'm leaving."

There was a loud smashing of windows a few rooms away, and then a chorus of howls. The four closest to me formed a wall protectively before me. The others took up stances like they were ready to run.

"You led them to us," hissed Isiak as he looked at Tessa.

"Impossible! This is why we took a car. He wasn't even around when I went to get Rai," exclaimed Tessa.

33

"This is all a dream," I muttered and backed away.

A pack of six, massive wolves tore into the dining hall. Their maws were coated in blood. I closed my eyes and sat in a corner muttering to myself.

"You fool! They aren't hurt," Tessa shouted.

There were some yelps from the wolves, a lot of growls from all sides, and I remember nothing after that.

I came to in my bed with Tessa standing on one side, and Ash on the other. The tension in the air was so palpable that even in my groggy state, I could feel it.

"I had the weirdest nightmare. Large dogs, vampires, the works," I grumbled.

They both looked at the floor.

"Guys…why are you hovering over me? What happened? I don't remember anything. Well, I don't know what was real and what was part of the nightmare anyway," I said.

"None of it was a dream, nightmare, or hallucination," said Tessa, "You had a panic attack and lost consciousness. We were so worried, it even stopped the fighting."

"Why is Ash here then?" I asked.

"I was home when she brought you in," Ash said quickly as Tessa opened her mouth to speak, "She told me something bad happened and I've been worried sick."

The trouble with knowing someone for a lifetime is that you just know when they are lying. The only truthful thing he said was that he was worried. I glared at him, and the look in his eyes told me he knew I knew he was lying about something. It also told me to let it go. But I was not going to.

"Tessa, what really happened?" I asked as I turned away from Ash.

"Well…uh…it's hard to say," said Tessa.

"Everyone out now," I said coldly, "And don't come back to talk to me until you decide to tell me the truth about things."

"My family isn't the normal kind. We were all turned by someone, who was also turned by someone. The one who turns us is our father. Any others they turn become our siblings. That's why Isiak is my uncle, because the one who turned me and him were turned by the same vampire. Corri is just someone that Isiak married that was part of a different family. Which in turn expanded our family and theirs," Tessa explained with a heavy sigh.

"Vampires do not exist," I growled.

"Yes, they do. And they are ruthless killers," Ash spoke up.

"Not all of us. My family isn't," said Tessa. "It would be a hard lifestyle to maintain when we stay places. Most vampires prefer to have servants that they can feed from and keep alive. It's the darker of our kin that you refer too."

"Your so-called cousins," Ash said with finger quotes as he said cousins, "tried to feed on my friends and me. They were too stupid to realize what we were."

"We can still get drunk and do stupid things. It might take a lot more alcohol than most, but it's possible. And they were hammered by the time they left with you. They had been drinking whiskey by the bottles. They couldn't smell the wolf on you because of that."

"Wolf on him? Did you train those wolves? They were huge," I murmured.

"That isn't exactly what she means…"

"Then what does she mean?"

In an instant, Ash had changed into a Teen Wolf

looking creature, the Michael J Fox version, then back to his normal self.

"We have three forms. Human, hybrid, wolf. When we're young, it happens without our ability to control it during the full moon cycle. As we age, it gets easier to control so that we can keep our senses, but we are still subject to the moon cycle. Some, when they reach adulthood, as we have recently, can change willingly and are not bound to the moon, like I did. Others can resist the pull and not change during the full moon, while also being unable to change whenever they wish and can basically just live as normal humans," explained Ash, "It was why I am always gone for that cycle. I cannot control myself when the moon is full."

I stared at him with shock written all over my face.

"I'm still dreaming," I muttered and pinched myself.

I grimaced as I drew blood. Tessa's emerald eyes went crimson, and she stared at my arm.

"Get out!" Ash growled at her.

In an instant, I heard the front door slam, and she was gone.

"You cannot trust their kind," sighed Ash.

"I'm not dreaming…am I?"

"I am afraid not, Ms. O'Neil," Ash said in his best impression of an old wise ninja master.

I rolled my eyes at him and groaned, "Now is not the time to quote ancient movies."

"It is always time to quote great movies. But seriously, look there is something strange about you. As a wolf, we have a predatory sense, and from you I have never had that. It's why you're my best friend. You don't tick any of my senses. And from what the other creatures were saying, it is the same for vampires. They don't notice you because you don't smell like food to them."

"Didn't look like I wasn't food when she had to leave so quickly," I said defeatedly.

"Fresh blood in the air. You can't say a shark is evil if you throw blood everywhere near it."

"What's so special about me? I'm nothing."

"You've never been nothing. Though, the what you are, I don't know. I recently found out my parents have been trying to figure that out since we met. Your parents do not have that same thing going on."

"Why would they?" I asked with a raised brow.

"They thought it was a bloodline..." Ash trailed off.

"Yea, dude. I was adopted from a church. Remember that?"

He slapped his forehead, "I'm an idiot. I forgot my parents never knew... I never bothered to mention that to them because your parents never told you."

"Idiot," I said affectionately.

"We need to find your real parents."

"I have my real parents. But I understand what you meant. How are we meant to do that though? They were never seen."

"Lucky for you, you've made friends with the oldest vampire I've ever seen," said Ash.

"Yujin?"

"Was that his name? Tessa's uncle?"

"Uh...that is Isiak. There was an older one there also," I said, confused. "A great-great grandfather."

"What? But that one next to you was at least a thousand years old."

"Though I don't know if he was Tessa's great-great or Isiak's. They both called him that," I mused.

"He's way older than that. He's supposed to be one of the first. Not an original, if such a thing truly exists, but as old as man itself. He could have been one of the first homo sapiens for all I know," Tessa said from my doorway.

"They all died…," said Ash, "The first werewolves wiped them all out."

"So your legends say. But if so, how would I exist?" questioned Tessa.

"That is a good point," I said.

Ash hmphed but said nothing.

"Do you think Isiak, or Yujin, would know of others like me?" I asked.

"My uncle doesn't. He didn't believe me about you. Nobody really speaks to my grandfather though. He shouldn't even have been there," said Tessa.

"Well, then let's go ask while he's around," I said as I stood up out of bed.

Chapter Seven

Before long, I was standing in front of the mansion, still in awe of its size.

"This is not smart," Ash said for the hundredth time.

"Duly noted," I said annoyed, "You don't have to come."

"Someone has to protect you," said Ash.

"Without your alpha? You can't fight the house alone. You killed good people," growled Tessa.

Ash just looked away.

"Alpha? Wait, Ash, isn't? Everyone seems to follow him," I said.

"I'm young. No chance am I ready to be an alpha. I'm just better at control... outside of that zenith of the full moon. When I can control myself, then maybe I will be ready to be an alpha."

As we approached the door, it swung open. Rafael stood at the door.

"Hello again, Master Ulfr," Rafael said towards Ash.

"He knows you?" I whispered.

"We know everyone Master Wentzel chooses to associate with, Master Eckles," said Rafael, "Lord Yujin is expecting all three of you."

We glanced at each other as he gestured for us to come in. Ash went in first, Tessa then pushed me in second, and she brought up the rear. It felt like they had put me in the middle of them to protect me. As Rafael led us through the maze of a house, I didn't see anyone else. We went up four flights of stairs, down hallways the length, then the width of the house, like the maze it was. I was confused when we stopped at what was just a small, cracked wooden door. Rafael opened it and stood to the side so we could enter. Inside was just as mundane, especially compared to the rest of the house. It was a small room, lit by candles, with a musky earthen smell. Sitting in the only chair, also quite simple and wooden, was Yujin.

"Welcome back, Rai," said Yujin with a large grin.

Tessa and Ash stood in front of me, and I had to squeeze by them in the small room.

"Hello, Yujin," I said, "So, I guess you know why I've come?"

"Yes, I do. My foolish offspring would have killed themselves on you," Yujin said cryptically.

"What do you mean?" I asked.

"There is a reason we don't see you as food. Because you are not food. Your blood is anathema to us. It cannot nourish us, too much will kill us, and we cannot turn you to one of us. I've tried it a few times to make certain," said Yujin.

"But I felt the bloodlust when I saw his blood earlier," spoke up Tessa.

"That is brought up by the sight, not smell, of blood. It is the same way a human can have their mouth water by seeing a steak on those fancy boxes you watch," laughed Yujin.

"Oh," she said and looked down.

"So, then what am I?" I asked.

"Wouldn't you rather figure that out for yourself?"

asked Yujin.

"No!" yelled all three of us.

"The youth… you are all so impatient," Yujin said with a wave of his hand and a sigh.

"Look, I just found out I'm some unknown freak, that vampires exist, and my best friend is only my friend because he doesn't view me as prey. Forgive me if I don't want to search for and find out more surprises later," I said exasperated.

"Yes, yes. These scions have always been hard-headed," said Yujin.

"Scions?" exclaimed Tessa.

"It does explain some things," mused Ash.

"What does that even mean?" I asked.

"The children of gods. Demigods, scions, half-bloods. Whatever you wish to call them. Heracles is the most famous of them, but there are usually hundreds of them at any given time," said Yujin.

"Hercules? But I don't have any powers. I'm not super strong or anything," I said.

"Of course not. He had none of those abilities he is portrayed with by these modern-day historians and mythology researchers. It doesn't make you all that special. You are so, very, spectacularly, human in every way. Except werewolves don't think of you as timid creatures they can kill at any time, vampires cannot smell you and don't view you as cattle to eat, and magic is useless on you."

"Magic? Magic exists?"

"I've never seen any proof of that myself," Ash said skeptically.

"You literally put up a warding spell in my room," I said with a laugh.

"Oh, magic is very much real. Not as flamboyant as movies would make it, but able to kill or awe. Disappear into thin air, create an aneurysm in an enemy, make fire out of air. You can do a lot with it, but it costs a great deal on the caster. So much that very few people have ever existed that could do more than petty parlor tricks," said Yujin.

"There hasn't been a true user since, Harry," muttered Tessa.

"Harry?" I asked.

"Houdini," answered Tessa.

"No way."

"He was very hardheaded. Went about looking until he found true magic. Or so I've heard," said Tessa.

"How old are you?" I asked.

"Twenty-four."

"How long have you been twenty-four?"

"For six months. That's kinda how time works. You don't just stop counting the years from going by just because I was turned at sixteen," Tessa said as she rolled her eyes.

"What? You're not five hundred? Isiak, said…"

"Isiak, was playing with you to get to me. But it went over your daft head," Tessa said with a smile as she pushed me with her shoulder.

"Oh."

"I could have told you she was a young one," Ash said with his head cocked at me.

"This is too much. I…I need to go," I muttered.

"As you wish scion," said Yujin.

The door behind us creaked open and Rafael held it open, waiting.

"Thank you," I said before I turned to leave.

Chapter Eight

For the next few weeks, I avoided Ash at home and ignored Tessa's texts and calls. I didn't want to believe in a world where monsters existed. Humanity had enough of those by itself, without vampires or werewolves killing us. But as life is the worst most days, it wouldn't let me forget so easily. One of my classes decided to start studying vampire bats. The school was in a tither about wolves prowling the streets. A magic show was announced. Luckily for me, I was not one people talked to, so I could steer myself away into isolation. My worst mistake, as it would turn out.

I had spent a late night in the library, my normal these days. The moon was full, so I knew Ash would be gone for a few days. I could still feel his presence at home, however, so I stayed out as much as possible. I wound my way toward the beach as I looked up at the stars. I felt lonelier than I had in years. As I stood at the water's edge, bemoaning my existence, I barely registered the sound of shuffling in the sand behind me.

The growl and hot, putrid breath on my neck was all that alerted me to the dangers around me. On instinct, I ducked down and rolled forward. I came up and turned to face a creature covered in seaweed. Clumps of its skin were missing that showed only bones, and it was completely naked. Luckily, the pelvis was part of his skin missing, showing only bone.

"Zombies?" I yelled, "Nobody told me about
43

zombies!"

It stumbled towards me, and I tried to run, but tripped over my own feet in the wet sand and water. I turned onto my back and looked up as a large, tawny colored wolf slammed into the water-logged zombie. In moments, it was ripped to shreds, and the mammoth beast, with its golden eyes, stared at me. It had an all too human rage in them as it hunched down and stalked around me. I scrambled to my feet as I followed it with my eyes.

"Ash? Is that you?" I asked in a trembling voice.

A snarl was my only reply. There was a look of confusion in that anger. Like he couldn't understand why he hadn't just ripped me to shreds like the creature now behind me.

"Buddy? You can't bite me. You'll only hurt yourself. Well, and me too, I guess. Okay, you'll only hurt both of us…I don't know how any of this works, Ash," I mumbled.

I stepped forward and his hackles raised, and a low growl formed in his throat.

"Calm down, Ash. You know me, you know my scent, right?" I asked and reached my hand out slowly.

He snapped out but didn't touch me. He wanted to bite me, I knew it, but also something inside him pulled him back from doing it. I don't know if it was my smell or what, but I moved a step closer. Then I realized my mistake immediately. A paw the size of my torso, claws extended, slammed into me. I flew limply through the air and slid a few feet in the sand when I finally landed. The last thing I remembered before waking up in the hospital was Ash kneeling next to me, his mouth moving. But I heard nothing as the darkness overtook me.

When I opened my eyes, everything was so bright

and white. For a moment, I thought I was at the pearly gates, though when everything finally came into focus, I saw ceiling tiles and heard the hum of machinery. Then came the pain.

"Take it easy," I heard the soothing voice of Ash as he laid a large hand on my shoulder.

"Why does it all hurt?" I cried.

"You're lucky you even survived," Ash said solemnly.

I turned my head despite the pain to see him wiping at his eyes.

"It's not your fault," I said.

"Yes, it is. I should have locked myself up. I just didn't trust the vampires to not attack. I waited too long before I attempted to lock myself up and turned before I could do it."

"Without you, I'd be dead anyway. How long have you been here?"

"A week… Doctors weren't sure you would ever wake up."

"Guess they don't know the powers of a scion," I joked.

I immediately regretted it, as the pain from even the smallest chuckle was too much for me.

"Take it easy," Ash said softly.

"Did you… bring me here?" I asked once the pain subsided.

"Yea. Something strange happened that I have never thought possible before. I was not only able to snap back into control, but also shed my wolf form at the zenith of the moon. I have been too worried about you to even ask my parents about that."

"Oh, God! Did you call my parents?"

"No, I didn't even think too."

"Thank God. I don't want them worried."

"Rai, I'm just really happy you're awake," Ash said as he squeezed my hand.

"Don't go getting all sappy on me…" I said, trying to keep the tremble out of my voice as I turned my head away.

After a long silence, it was broken by a growl from my stomach.

"Hungry?" laughed Ash.

"A little," I muttered, my face red.

"Stay here, I'll go get a snack."

"Oh yes, I was planning on moving away the second you left," I said with an eyeroll.

His smile made me get even more red.

It was about a month in the hospital, so by the time I got home, I was so excited to make real food. I still hadn't seen or heard from Tessa that whole time I was in the hospital. I didn't even know if she knew I had been hurt. To make things worse, I didn't even know why a zombie attacked me. But all that was in the back of my mind as I started to make my first meal in what seemed like forever.

"Did you ever ask your parents how you were able to start controlling your form during the full moon?" I asked Ash as he walked in on me making dinner.

"No," Ash said too quickly and turned away.

It was another full moon, and here he was, just hanging out like a normal person. He could still transform. He did it earlier when he left with his pack to just run and burn some energy. I had finally realized that all the people who had stayed around Ash were other werewolves also. They hadn't been part of surfing teams or whatever else he had told me. One of the teachers at the college was their acting Alpha also. From what I gathered it was to keep them in that pack mentality while also from in-fighting to become that pack alpha. I still didn't quite understand it all, and it was too much for me to wrap my head around. He had made it back for dinner, a very late-night dinner. I put the chicken in the oven and shuffled over to him.

"You do know you can't lie to me, right?" I asked.

"But I can lie to myself just fine," he murmured.

"Talk to me," I said, and turned him to face me.

He looked down and to the right since he towered over me. I gently turned his face to mine.

"What's going on?" I asked softly.

"It seems my parents can do the same thing I can. It is an incredibly unique thing, and it rarely happens. When it does it usually involves two wolves though," he began, "Apparently it's something that happens involving a person you love…"

"Wha…wha…," I stammered, unable to create a sentence.

As he leaned down, there was a pounding on the door. We both jerked back, and I winced in pain. We both stared at the door as the knocking grew more insistent.

"Expecting anyone?" we both asked.

After a laugh, Ash made his way over to answer.

"He…" started Ash as he opened the door.

Tessa ducked under his arm and went by him before he could react. One second nobody was next to me, and then she was there. I blinked rapidly and stared at her.

"Are you okay? What happened? Who did this?" She just started blurting out questions as she looked me over and circled me.

She stopped, then turned to Ash as if it had just dawned on her what time of the month it was.

"How can you be here? Standing there like that?" she

asked.

"What are you doing here?" he snarled as his eyes turned golden.

"Down boy. Isiak had me sent away. I just returned after my great-great grandfather told me to. Isiak was overruled. I tried to tell Rai, but he never answered me."

"Sorry… I was avoiding Ash, also. It was too much for me to take," I said softly.

"One of our doctors mentioned that you had been hurt badly and were recently released. I rushed over the moment I heard," she said as she circled me again.

I was wrapped in bandages, I thought I looked like a mummy. As she got back in front of me, her eyes softened, and she hugged me tightly.

"Ow," I groaned.

"Sorry! Sorry!" she yelped.

"It's fine," I squeaked.

"Who did this? What happened? Nobody could tell me."

"A zombie attacked me," I said.

"Are you sure?" she asked skeptically.

"Well, it was rotting. There were a lot of bones showing. It was so very, very dead. So that's what I would call it."

"I've never heard of zombies being real. I've seen some things… The power it would take to create one with necro magic is intense," mumbled Tessa.

She paced around the room in deep thought.

"Well, you weren't there then, so go away now," said Ash as he held open the door.

"Not by choice. And I am here now."

"We don't need your kind."

48

"Sit boy. I know dogs are loyal, but back off."

They were right next to each other and glared at one another. Ash towered over Tessa, but she wasn't backing down. His eyes were golden, and her eyes were crimson. I stepped between them and pushed them away from each other.

"This isn't helping anything," I said angrily.

"Neither will she!"

Tessa went to respond, but I held up my hand to stop her.

"No. Both of you stop now," I sighed.

Ash turned away and slammed the door on his way out. A few seconds later, a loud howl was heard as he ran away.

"I'm sorry. I didn't mean to antagonize him and get out of control. I was just worried when I heard. What if something like that happens again?" Tessa said, her eyes filled with water.

"It's fine. Let's just sit down," I said wearily.

She helped me to the couch.

"Are you cooking?" she asked.

"Yea. It's got a few hours to go still," I said.

She turned on a movie and, with my expert tutelage, finished making dinner. Ash still hadn't returned by the time she left. Though I guess he would have been able to smell if she were still here or not. I felt a bit guilty because I was happy he didn't return. It was nice just me and her having dinner together after so long. The food wasn't half-bad either. A little blander than I would have made it, but she was a beginner, so I couldn't complain much.

"You could stay," I said as she got up to leave.

"I wish I could. I would love to. But the sun is a real

killer on my complexion," she joked.

She kissed me on the cheek, turned red, and was gone in an instant as I stared dumbfounded in the doorway. I still stood there when Ash came back.

Chapter Nine

"I'm not discussing this," I said as I tied my shoes. "I'm going to class. You should too."

Ash seethed as he returned to his room, but I heard him getting clothes together. He was mad because it was the weekend, and I had plans to spend it with Tessa. Though tonight I wasn't spending the time with her here, so he could stay home if he wanted to. Before I was even halfway down the block, he caught up with me.

"I can't protect you if you keep being foolish," said Ash.

"Maybe I don't need protecting."
He eyed my still bandaged body.
"Okay, point taken. But not from her of all people."

"I don't trust her kind."

"Then TRUST me."

"I do," he said timidly.

"You won't even talk about the other night, when I was making dinner."

"It doesn't matter," he said quickly and sped up his pace.

I growled at him and slowed my own speed.

"I'll talk to you tomorrow," I called out.

I half expected him to shift and run away with his tail tucked. Classes went by slower than ever, but eventually I was back home and getting ready to meet Tessa. I didn't want to mention it to Ash, but I was going to meet Yujin before I went to her. She was meant to meet me at the diner we had gone to that first night, but I was waiting for Jeffery to pick me up. Going back to that house scared me, especially since I was going to be there alone. But, I needed to do it that way. Ash and Tessa would probably have tried to stop me. After I had finished changing the bandages, there was a soft knock on the door.

"Give me a minute," I called out.

"Take your time," came Rafael's voice from the other side.

I froze. Why was he here? Confusion slowed me more than pain, but I finally made it to the door. Rafael stood beside two men who carried a coffin.

"No. No. No," I protested.

"Do invite us in," came Yujin's voice from the coffin.

"Why are you here? How do you know where I live?" I asked.

"I told you we know everything, Master Eckles," Rafael said as he walked by me and started closing curtains. He then walked back into the hall and got blinders to block out the sun completely.

"This will be much easier to answer if you let me in," said Yujin.

"If I don't?"

"Then you have angered a powerful being who knows exactly where you live. Who also has the answers to questions that nobody else will ever have."

"You're invited in, Yujin," I said against my better judgment.

"Thank you."

The two men carried the coffin across my threshold.

"You can come out now master," said Rafael.

"Why is he here?" I asked and pointed to Rafael.

"He is, what you mortals call, my Renfield."

I stared cluelessly at Yujin as he sat up in the coffin.

"You young ones have no sense of culture," sighed Yujin, "He is my human to do things in the day that I desire. When I have no such desires, he butlers for Isiak."

"Oh," I said. "Well, welcome to my humble abode."

"Humble indeed. It smells of wet dog," Yujin said as he glanced around.

"Don't make me regret this," I sighed, "Why did you come here?"

"Why? Too see the splendor in which you gods choose to live," mocked Yujin.

"Leave."

"Can't take jokes I see. Guess you don't wish to find your lineage either."

"You know?" I asked wide-eyed.

"Me? Oh no. But I know how to find out. Also, you can find out why a zombie attacked you."

"Does everyone know about that?" I cringed.

"I take it very seriously to keep track of people who can kill me. Like that Mr. Ulfr. He never strays too far from you when you are near Tessa."

"He's been following me?"

"Oh yes. I bet even little Tessa doesn't know. He is a gifted fellow himself. I bet he's watching Isiak's house right now."

"No, no, no. Stop trying to make me mad at Ash. Who can tell me who I am?"

"Well, what better place to start than the church you were found at?"

"I've already thought of that, but, my parents told me

53

nobody knows how I got there."

"Sure. Have you tried going there yourself though?"

"No…but…"

"But what? Too far? Not for Tessa to achieve. School? Your loyal dog gets out plenty. Or is it plain old-fashioned fear?"

"Look, fear is healthy," I muttered.

"Yes. It is. That is why I've outlived my brothers and sisters. They had all that precious arrogance, and superiority complexes, yet they had none of that small little thing called fear. I prefer a dose of it all."

"Is that all? To go back to the beginning? I don't even know any names."

"I have my own interests in this. But I also want to see how you children do with this search. I have grown bored and need a bit of amusement."

"Oh great. So, you expect me to fail," I said and rolled my eyes.

"I expect great things from my sources of amusement," Yujin said with a smile.

Chapter Ten

It was hours after Yujin left, and I sat on my couch, lost in thought. It was my phone that brought me back to reality when it rang.

"Hello?" I answered absently.

"Are you okay? Where are you? Did someone hurt you?" came Tessa's worried voice.

"Huh?"

"We were meant to meet an hour ago."

"What? I swear it's only been a few minutes since he left."

"Him?"

I looked at the time and did a double take.

"Sorry! I'll be right there," I apologized.

"It's fine. I will meet you halfway, and you can tell me what happened."

I quickly went out the door and made my way towards her. Soon we were walking along the beach.

"Your grandfather came to my house. I was meant to meet him at your house after you had left. For some reason he surprised me and showed up as I was getting ready," I said.

"What?!" yelled Tessa, "You tried to meet great-great grandfather without me around? Nobody can predict what he will do. The wrong word and he could have killed you!"

"This is why I didn't tell you. I needed to know what he knows about me. Apparently, he knows nothing, but he did tell me how to find out."

55

"What did he say?" Tessa asked softly.

"That I need to go back to the church I was left at," I sighed. "But, I'm worried. And a bit scared."

"What's to be scared of?"

"Have you seen some of those godly legends? They are terrible people. They kill people just because they can. They kidnap people, do unspeakable things I don't even want to say. They are all crazy. What if my godly parent is the worst creature imaginable? What if they make someone like Yujin seem like an angel."

"Legends are not real, doofus. And who your parent is will never change who you are," she said and wrapped her arm around my elbow.

"Maybe. But what if they make me immortal? What if I am immortal? I don't think I could watch my parents die while I stay looking young. Or even worse, watching Ash grow old as I stay the same age. Then he dies and I just continue on living."

"But I wouldn't die," she said softly and leaned closer to me.

I looked down at her and stared into her eyes. Time seemed to stop, and I felt my heart skip a beat.

"Then I guess there would be upsides," I grinned.

"I do understand that fear though. It's why I... my kind never become attached to others. Usually. It's hard to think of their mortality while being attached to them. And to turn them, to make them live this life... It's a hard choice. Plus, they smell of food, and fighting that urge when you're around someone all the time. It's hard," she muttered and pulled away.

I wanted to pull her back and tell her that I would never leave her. That I would always be around for her.

But, I knew it would be a lie. As far as I knew, I could die at any moment for a variety of reasons. She was effectively immortal, and I hadn't even contemplated that. I would grow older and older. She would continue to look as beautiful as she had the moment I met her. She only had to worry about the sunlight, wood, werewolves…and me.

"Will you go with me?" I asked hesitantly.

"Of course!" she beamed, "We can get my driver and car. Since you know… the sun. We can leave whenever you want."

"Ash has to come also."

Her nose wrinkled, but she said, "Figured as much. Fine, it can be done. If he agrees to get along with me also."

"Thanks," I whispered and slipped my hand into hers.

The steel of her lip ring was cool in the night air as she pressed her lips to mine. I don't know if I was too hot or what, but her lips felt warm on mine as she kissed me. It was over too quickly. A quick peck, and I wanted more. The taste of her lips lingered on, but she looked down and away and I resigned myself to settle with what I had and nothing more.

"Sorry," she muttered.

"Don't be," I said, "I enjoyed it."

She nudged my shoulder and laughed, "So did I."

We held hands as we walked on the moonlit beach as the water licked at our feet.

Chapter Eleven

"No," said Ash, his blue eyes ablaze.

"You'll just follow anyway," I said with an eyeroll. "So come on and just agree already,"

"I am not letting you go halfway across the country with that… thing," growled Ash.

"SHE has a name, Ashlan."

"IT is no better than that zombie who attacked you."

"Can't you just spend a few days being civil? For my sake? So I can find out what, and who, I am?"

"We can go together without their help. Their help always comes with a cost."

"This is not a discussion. You can come or stay," I sighed. "But, I am going with Tessa."

As I turned to head down the hallway, he suddenly grabbed my shoulder and pinned me against the wall with a firm hand. My heart raced as his lips pressed forcefully against mine, catching me completely off guard. His body pressed tightly against me, his hands moving to grip my waist as I melted into the kiss. My fingers entwined in his hair, pulling him closer as our passion grew. His kisses trailed down my neck, sending shivers down my spine. I pushed him away, my breathing heavy and labored.

"No," I gasped, trying to catch my breath. "If you bite me too hard, it could be bad."

His eyes blazed with desire, his chest rising and falling heavily as he reluctantly pulled away. Leaning in once more, I

58

placed a hand on his chest to stop him.

"Not now," I whispered, feeling the electricity between us. "I can't."

"Felt like you could a second ago," he purred.

"I got lost in the moment…" I frowned. "You can't change my mind this way. It's already made up."

He backed up as his eyes turned back to that tantalizing blue.

"I'm not going," was all he said before he turned away and went into his room.

I leaned against the wall and sighed, my heart pounding and my breathing tight. He was so annoying sometimes.

Chapter Twelve

I decided to wait until summer break to leave. Which… was not the best for Tessa, but she didn't object. I took my suitcase, threw it into the trunk of a long limo, and sat in the back along with her. Our driver, who she called Beka, set out on our journey from SoCal to Central Oklahoma on a warm night.

"Is he really not coming?" Tessa asked as I got in alone.

"He refused. No matter how many times I asked him," I said dejectedly.

She scooted against me, and I laid my head on her shoulder. Soon I was asleep. I woke up slightly as I felt her move away from me. Through blurred vision, I saw her climb into the front of the limo through the now rolled down window partition. There was an audible gasp, and I fell back asleep. When I woke up, the tinted windows were up, the sun visible behind it, and my head was in her cool lap. She had a miniskirt on, and she looked lifeless as she sat there, her eyes closed. I sat up and went to touch her shoulder when a voice snapped at me.

"Don't!" Beka yelled.

My hand stopped inches from Tessa's shoulder.

"I wasn't doing anything," I hmphed. "I was making sure she was alive."

"She isn't alive," Beka said matter-of-factly. "And never touch a vampire in stasis. If you want to live anyway."

60

There was a bandaged stained red that poked out of the top of her turtleneck.

"What happened?" I asked.

"What do you mean?"

"Your neck?"

"Nothing is wrong with my neck," she said robotically.

She shook her head as if to wake up.

"Sorry. That happens when somebody tries to talk about bites," Beka said. "It's an automatic thing that gets implanted into our subconscious during the time we are made to become blood banks."

I climbed into the passenger seat.

"So, how do you drive and not sleep? Is it because of her?" I asked.

"Huh? No, I'm still human. I'm just drinking lotsa caffeine," Beka said and pointed to a bag next to her. "It's only a twenty-four-hour drive. I'll be able to sleep when we get there. Until then, red bulls. Lots of red bulls."

"Are the vampires nice to you?" I asked.

"What do you mean?"

"My friend seems to think they are incapable of true human emotions. That they only want to feed on us and we're nothing but steaks to them. Isiak wanted to turn me after meeting me. Yujin is beyond frightening, but he is helping me. It might be for his own amusement, but that implies human emotions to an extent. I don't know what to think. This is too overwhelming for me most of the time and I have nobody human to talk about with this stuff."

Beka looked over her shoulder at the still form of Tessa before she spoke.

"They, mostly, view us as livestock. Occasionally

one of the 'donors' gets taken a liking to and then they are transformed. After that they can no longer trigger the animal inside. It hardly ever works out after that. They become equals and… their power dynamic is not the same. The one who was changed no longer feels beholden to the one who changed them. Some of the times, the one who changed them grows bored without that feeling of power over them. Isiak, and Corri, seem to be an exceedingly rare exception. But they were already vampires when they met, even if Corri was newer. Tessa is nice but she keeps her distance from everyone. Even from her so-called family. With you though, she has a different air about her. I've been with her since she was sixteen and I've never seen her happy. Until now that is. She cannot deny what she is though, and if you cannot accept everything that comes with it then you need to leave."

"That doesn't answer me."

"She's not a killer, but she is not human. That is what you should never forget. Our moral standards are not like hers. To cows, us humans would seem the same as they do to us. She might remember the time she was mortal, and one of us. But time will eventually overwrite that. That humanity you see in her might not stay the older and further she is removed from that old life."

"Oh," I said as I looked back at Tessa.

"If you want to be awake when she is, you should try to get more sleep. It's still another twelve hours until we get to our destination."

"I'm fine. So how long have you worked with, been with, uh, whatever with them?"

"It's always a forced recruitment," Beka said flatly. "I've been with the family since I was a young girl. Around eight."

I looked horrified at her.

"Tessa's father had no qualms about age, race, or anything. He found me in an orphanage, took me in, and forced me to train to be a protector during the day and a source of food during the night. Then when he felt me adequate enough for whatever standards he had set, he created Tessa."

"That sounds terrible…"

"Gregory was not a great individual by normal standards. It was what ultimately caused his death by others of his kind. He was tolerant to those he valued, and if he saw you as a waste he would disregard you as nothing but a pawn. I was treated better by him, because of what he was, than when I had been at the orphanage or other foster homes. I made sure I stayed on his good side so that I would not be sent back there."

"I'm in way over my head," I said.

"Not any more than us humans are on a normal basis."

We rode in silence until sundown. Then I went back into the back as Tessa began to stir.

"Good morning," I said with a smile.

She opened her eyes and looked at me. Her eyes were a darker crimson and filled with hunger. She blinked and her eyes were back to emerald. They twinkled as she smiled brightly at me.

"Good evening. I hope Beka was not too much of a bore," joked Tessa.

"Never am," Beka said dryly.

A few minutes later, we stopped at a gas station.

"Can you pay for the fuel? And get me more red bulls?" Beka asked and handed me a credit card, "Fifty in the tank. The biggest can they have. Get yourself something to snack on."

As I walked away and looked back, I saw Tessa climbing into the front seat.

Chapter Thirteen

The first thing we did when we got to Perry, Oklahoma was find a hotel. I had expected to find a rundown place that didn't ask questions. Where we ended up was a nice-looking Holiday Inn. It doesn't sound fancy, but in a town with barely five thousand people, it was decent. I wanted to start immediately, but it was extremely late. Tessa pointed out to me that everything in town was closed, which probably included the church. So, she convinced me to get some rest with her.

The room had two king-sized beds. As soon as we had taken everything out of the car, Beka passed out. She splayed out on one of the beds, taking up the whole thing now that she was able to finally get to sleep. Tessa pulled me over to the other bed by the window.

"Won't this be dangerous?" I asked as she pulled me onto the bed.

"It will be fine. I promise I won't bite," she joked. "As long as I am prepared to be touched when I go into stasis, it'll be fine. Just hold me."

She was cold as she curled against my body. Her hand pressed against my stomach under my shirt. It was nice against the heat of the night, and my rising body temperature. I fell asleep easier than I thought. I woke up with her face buried in my neck, and her right arm and leg sprawled over me. I wrapped my arms around her and felt content to stay where I was. I looked towards Beka, but she wasn't in her bed. She wasn't anywhere in the room as I looked around.

As I laid there, my mind began to wander. What if she was dead? What if something happened to her when she went out? What if she was the one who sent the zombies after me? What if she wanted to keep me away from Tessa?

There was a bang on the door, and I jumped up as I pushed Tessa off me. The door handle jiggled, and I hid on the backside. It cracked open, and a tall figure creeped through. The fading light nearly touched Tessa as the door opened before it closed. I jumped at the figure, who spun around and planted me face first on the floor.

"What are you doing?" barked Beka.

She held onto a large bag of fast-food tacos and glared down at me.

"I wish I knew," I groaned. "I thought you were dead, and whoever sent a zombie after me was coming."

She shook her head at me and stood up.

"Eat. She will be waking up soon, and then we can find this church," she said and handed me the bag.

I munched on a burrito from Taco Mayo and tried to remember the church name. It was like clockwork. As the last of the sun faded away, Tessa stirred on the bed.

"Oh, you left," Tessa said, a sadness in her voice.

"Only to play hero," joked Beka.

I looked at the ground and Tessa looked between us in confusion.

"Anyway, time to go to church. If I recall its Assembly of God. A two-story church down a dirt road. Off a main road on the outside of town," I said quickly to change the subject.

"Well then let's start," Tessa said, a pain still in her voice.

"You won't um…be hurt. Will you?" I asked.

"By a church? Hardly. These days they hardly have much religious power. So, unless it's a very devout pastor, I should be fine," said Tessa.

I stared at her with wide eyes.

"I'm joking!" she yelled with a laugh. "That rumor once again comes from the darker of my kin. Something inside them hates truly holy ground. Maybe it's psychological, or something even darker, I'm not sure. But it seems to be less and less effective from what I hear."

"Go start the car," Beka said as she tossed me the keys.

"Uhm…okay," I said.

A few minutes later, they came out and both sat in the back.

"Who is driving?" I asked.

"You are now," said Tessa, a hint of shame in her voice.

Beka looked paler than normal as I looked at her in the rear-view mirror.

"Is she okay?" I exclaimed.

"I'm… fine. Just… drive," she breathed heavily.

"What happened?" I asked.

Tessa just looked at the floor.

"Nothing. Go," ordered Beka.

She laid on a bench seat away from Tessa. I shrugged and took out my phone. Lucky for me, there was only one church by the name I was looking for in the town. Soon I was on my way, following a GPS. Nestled between a Mariachi Mexican Grill and a McDonalds was a small road. I turned down it, and a few minutes later we were coming up to a large, off-white building. The front half of it was taller than the back half. The parking lot was empty, except for a large four-by-four truck. Through the stained-glass windows, there was light visible in the main area.

"Guess we get lucky," I said. "Anyone going with me?"

"I will," Tessa said softly.

Inside, replacing old or ripped hymns with newer ones, was a person that didn't look like they would own the truck outside. He had short, white hair and walked stooped over at a slow pace. He had on a black suit. He could have been anywhere from 60 to 90 and would have been as tall as Tessa if he hadn't been stooped over. He looked fragile, as if a strong wind could pick him up and throw him for miles. He whistled to himself as he walked down the pews. After a moment, I cleared my voice loudly. He turned slowly towards us.

"Oh? I'm sorry. I was not expecting to see anyone here today," said the old man in a strong voice. "My name is, Pastor Thomas. Who might you be?"

"Uh, I'm Rai Eckles. This is my friend, Tessa Wentzel," I answered.

"Eckles? Hmm, that name rings a few bells in my addled old brain. What brings two young ones here? I don't do impromptu weddings, just so you know. I believe that is something that needs to be planned and discussed with all parties, parents included for ones so young," said Pastor Thomas.

"Something isn't right," Tessa whispered in my ear.

"No, no wedding," I said and felt my face turning red. "I'm just looking for someone that may not be here anymore."

Tessa positioned herself behind me and pressed her

hands flat against my back.

"Oh? Do you have a name? And is your friend okay?" asked Pastor Thomas.

"She's fine," I lied. "I'm not sure of his name to be honest. I was found here when I was a baby. I'm kinda on a pilgrimage to find my birth parents. I was hoping I could pick up the trail here."

"We don't get many of those here. Babies that have been left, that is. But I am the only one here who would have taken you in. I found a nice, young, barren couple who seemed like decent people."

"So, it was you?" I asked excitedly.

The claws in my back brought down my excitement as I winced.

"Very much so. I have been waiting for you to find me," said Pastor Thomas.

I looked at him and raised a brow.

"Your little plaything hasn't yet figured it out, Vampire?" asked Pastor Thomas.

"What haven't I? Wait! You know she's a vampire?" I exclaimed.

"We know our own. I knew what you were before I was turned into this. Now, I want you as my thrall," Thomas said as his eyes turned bright red.

Tessa whipped me into a pew, and Thomas tackled her.

"So young," Thomas said from on top of Tessa.

"You're not much older," grunted Tessa.

"Oh, I am old enough in this matter."

He picked her up by the face and threw her through one of the stained-glass windows. He then stood over me before I could move.

"Now I will have a godling on my side," Thomas said, and he came toward my neck.

I let out an ear-piercing scream as his fangs tore into my flesh. The world became darker as I felt my life draining from the blood being consumed by the creature on top of me.

Pastor Thomas pulled away from me with a look of agony written all over his face.

"What did you do to me?" he cried out.

Moments later, he turned to dust as a fire welled up inside me. It was so painful that it chased away the darkness edging on my vision, and I screamed out even louder with a pain worse than when my throat was ripped apart. Through the pain, I noticed Tessa was at my side. Her hands were covered in my blood. I tried to speak, to say anything about what was happening. I saw her mouth move, but I couldn't hear anything that came out as she talked rapidly. The fire spread through my body. Tessa jumped back as the fire within erupted and covered my body. It is a weird feeling to feel your body turn to ash.

Chapter Fourteen

I lay there in my own ashes, completely naked. My clothes had burned away with my body. Yet, I was here. Weak, but alive.

"I guess he didn't hear I was poison to him," I joked, my voice cracked and hoarse.

I looked over at Tessa and she was covered in my blood. Her eyes were the deepest red I had ever seen, and she stared at me in disbelief.

"Tessa? What happened? Am I here? Can you hear me?" I asked in a raspy voice.

She vanished before my eyes, and I sighed heavily.

"Guess I am dead. Just my luck, I don't even get to meet my godly parent in some weird afterlife," I muttered. "And I didn't think I would have a need for water in the afterlife."

I sat up with great effort as a ball of cloth flew through the broken window and landed near me. It took me a moment to realize it was balled-up clothes for me to put on. So, I guess I was alive after all. As I undid the ball, I groaned. The shirt was an ugly yellow shirt with pink polka dots on it, and the pants were too small yoga pants. It took longer than it should have to get dressed, because I was still in a lot of pain, and I felt like I had run a marathon. Slowly, I made my way outside to where Tessa stood, the blood cleaned off her. She was also in new clothes. A pair of cut-off pants and a sleeveless T-shirt.

"How are you alive?" she asked and wrapped me in a hug.

"Ow, ow, ow," I said, "You're going to break my ribs." She let me go and stepped back.

"Sorry," she frowned.

"I don't know what happened. I thought I was going to die. What am I?" I asked and leaned into her.

I wrapped my arms around her and buried my face into the crook of her neck. She gingerly wrapped her arms around me.

"I wish I knew. Great-great grandfather will probably know once we get back. But I'm worried he turned that man and that is why he sent you here. If not, we have bigger problems. Someone else knows you're a scion and left that man if you came looking for your past. They couldn't just be using this one in a million longshot, so if someone is looking for you, they will have other avenues to try and find you. Also, as much as I wish they could, a vampire cannot use magic. So, the zombie is still unanswered."

"So, this was all for nothing…" I whimpered, "I put you in danger for just more questions and we've learned nothing."

"More questions are good. Questions can eventually have answers. With questions, we can look for other things," Tessa said as she ran her fingers through my hair.

"I don't want you to get hurt because of something involving me," I said and hugged her tighter.

"I am harder to hurt than you think. Don't worry about me. I will help you find the answer to all this. I will always be here by your side."

Chapter Fifteen

I fell asleep as we started our way back to Cali. I felt the coldness of Tessa against me, but it did nothing to lighten my mood. I had learned nothing, been attacked again, and could have lost Tessa. All for what? Because of parents I didn't know? I was mad at them for leaving me. I was also mad at Ash for not being there to help.

It must have been night still when I was woken up from the pain of being thrown to the floor of the limo from a hard jarring as Tessa screamed. I then heard loud metal-on-metal scrapping and was whipped into the waiting arms of Tessa.

"What's going on?" I asked.

"Someone rammed us," Beka said coolly from the front, "They won't let up either."

"Who?" I asked.

Tessa looked at me with her mouth tensed. It was then I felt the blood on the back of my head from where I had hit it on the floor.

"Oh god," I said.

"It's fine," she said clearly not fine.

Her eyes were closed as she held me tightly, and the car rocked again. The back door window shattered inward, and I saw the edge of a yellow truck pulled away, the paint on it scrapped up. In the back of the truck, two people held onto the rails. In the cab, a burly old man was at the wheel.

"Wolves," growled Tessa.

73

"Werewolves?" I asked.

"I can smell them. Can you go faster, Beka!"

"Oh yes, faster. That's something I never thought of doing," muttered Beka.

Another ram sent the limo careening into a ditch. Tessa pulled me and Beka from the car as the truck stopped down the road from us.

"Get ready to run," whispered Tessa.

She stood in front of us, and the werewolves walked towards us. The burly, beer-gutted driver was leading the pack of three. The two behind him were no older than eighteen, if even that. But they were tall, well over six feet, and rail thin.

"Well boys, what do we have here?" the beer gut said to the other two in a heavy southern drawl.

"A bloodsucker and her ghouls. We get to have fun tonight, right Pa?" asked the left one.

"That we do, Jethro," said Pa as he transformed into hybrid form.

His two sons did the same. I heard a feral growl escape Tessa, and she scooted closer to me.

"I am not going to leave you," said Beka.

"Don't be stupid. Rai can't protect himself. Take them, and get out of here," said Tessa.

"Nobody gets to leave," said Pa, "Go left, Jethro. Billy Bob, go right."

They spread out in a circle as they came forward. I looked at them in horror. We were going to die. I couldn't do a thing to stop it. Once again. Some demi-god I had turned out to be. Billy Bob flew into his brother as I turned to face the Jethro wolf. I turned back to see a ten-foot wolf on its hind legs. Its fur was a tawny color, and rage filled its golden eyes.

"What are you doing, boy?" Pa asked, his voice and eyes raged to match those of the massive wolfman.

"Leave now, and nobody gets hurt worse," growled Ash.

"You ain't from 'round these parts. This is my territory, and nobody tells me what to do on my property. These three creatures are mine to do with as I please," said Pa.

"I would love to, but someone would never forgive me if I did that. Please leave, I don't want to fight my own kind," Ash said, his voice losing the edge it had.

"Spoken like a welp and a loser. You're no alpha. How dare you speak to me like I should listen to you?" roared Pa.

He shifted into a form like Ash's but much shorter and thicker. As he attacked Ash, I noticed the other two in the same form but still smaller than Ash and going to surround him. Tessa noticed them also and was already moving. Pa smashed into Ash with enough force to rip an oak from the ground. Ash was braced for it and didn't budge. Tessa threw one of the young wolves into a tree and stared down the other.

"Stop this boy," grunted Pa as his muscles bulged under his graying fur.

"My friend is off limits," Ash growled as he strained against the power of the other, older wolf.

"Bloodsucker lover! I am gonna rip you apart," said Pa.

"Vamps can die for all I care, but they aren't one," said Ash as he pushed Pa back.

As I looked back at Tessa, she had ripped into Billy Bob's neck. He had turned back to human form, a glossy stare on his pale face. Beka turned me away as I saw Jethro charge at her.

"That is not a pretty sight. I don't want you to view her differently," said Beka.

I noticed she had also turned away, obviously not worried about Tessa. What happened next, I couldn't see, but soon Ash and Tessa stood in front of me covered in blood.

"I didn't need your help," scoffed Tessa.

"Same can be said of you. I saw those two coming. I could have stopped them without their deaths," growled Ash.

"Why are you here anyway?" snarled Tessa.

"To make sure Rai is safe," Ash said as he puffed out his chest.

"They are safe. With me."

"Didn't look like it from where I was."

"Stop! Both of you!" I yelled.

They turned toward me with vastly different expressions on their faces. Tessa seemed to shrink into herself, and Ash was dumbfounded.

"We need to get the car out of the ditch and get moving. No arguing because Ash, is being an idiot," I said.

Beka was already moving the good ole boys' truck into a position to pull the limo out of the ditch. Inside the truck were straps we attached to the limo, and we pulled it out with minimal effort. At least one of us was sensible. Once we were on our way, Ash and Tessa sat on opposite sides of the limo.

"Have you followed us all this way?" I asked with a side glance at Ash.

"Mostly. I couldn't follow you to the church. That area was too open. And what could have gone wrong there?"

"I was attacked by a vampire that was stronger than Tessa. I could have used your help then, too!" I scooted over and poked Ash in the chest, "If you're going to keep stalking me, then why were you not there when I needed you most."

He looked at me dumbfounded, "How... I."

"Yes, you didn't know. Because, you decided to be stubborn and run all the way here. You were too worried that Tessa would kill me, you never stopped to think something else would. There could have been a whole zombie horde in that church for all you know. You need to get over this prejudice. Tessa clearly doesn't think much of werewolves either, but she doesn't tell me to stay away from you."

"I don't view you as food to eat!" Ash said defensively.

"No, it's worse. You find us something small, scared, and not worth your time. All the friends you have are like you. You don't go outside your own species, even though at the bars you're clearly popular with even us normal humans."

"You are hardly a normal human," Beka said dryly.

"Not helping," I groaned.

"I'm sorry," murmured Ash. "You said a vampire was there, how did you survive? I guess that explains the weird clothes."

"We got lucky," I said and moved back to the middle bench seat with crossed arms.

Ash looked up at Tessa and sighed heavily, "I'm sorry."

Tessa eyes grew wide, and she jerked back.

"Uh, it's no issue. Sorry myself," she stammered.

"So did you find anything out at that church?" Ash asked as he looked back at me.

"Not really. It's just more questions. I need to talk to Yujin. He's the only person who can probably answer anything. The person who gave me to my parents is now dead," I sighed.

"I might be able to be fine with Tessa, but that one is too much. That one is immensely powerful and could kill all three of us in an instant," Ash said, using Tessa's name for the first time.

"Well, you're going to hate that he knows where we live and has access to our apartment," I said and drew into myself.

"What?!" exclaimed Ash.

"It was the only way he would talk to me…"

"I told them it was stupid too," Tessa said.

"You told her?!" yelled Ash.

"Well, you were being too stubborn to listen to anything I said!" I yelled.

"Don't make me turn this car around," came Beka's voice from the front.

"Not now, Beka," Tessa said with a groan and facepalm.

The rest of the ride was quiet. I went to sleep and when I woke up, I was in my bed. Still in the same too-small clothes.

Chapter Sixteen

I took a few days to recover. My energy was still low and, much to the displeasure of Tessa and Ash, I stood in front of Isiak's house. Rafael opened the door and ushered me in.

"Master had expected to see you sooner," Rafael said.

Ash and Tessa followed me in as I followed Rafael.

"Why did he think I would be seeing him?" I asked.

Rafael said nothing in response.

"You have to have some idea," I said.

He just kept walking.

"Well, that's not awkward at all," I said.

"Rafael isn't going to know the mind of great-great grandfather any more than I am," Tessa piped up.

It wasn't long before we were back in front of the crooked door.

"Master waits for you inside."

I opened the door and went in. Yujin sat there with a smug grin on his face.

"It seems you have made it back, young one," he said as I stormed in.

"With more questions and no answers. You're going to give me some of those," I said angrily.

"Watch that temper," warned Yujin as he suddenly stood before me, eye to eye.

I shrunk back as Ash and Tessa stood between me and Yujin.

"Now, what did you learn?" Yujin asked as he sat back in his chair.

"Nothing. Like I said, all I have is more questions."

"Which is part of learning. Without this latest information, how could you have those questions?" chided Yujin.

"The person waiting for me was a vampire," I began.

"And he was only a decade or so old," added Tessa, "He wasn't changed when Rai was born."

"Hmm," was all Yujin responded as he waited for me to continue.

"He said he had been waiting for me to return. He wanted to change me into a vampire. Someone gave him half the information or something. He bit me. Ripped out my throat. I should be dead. Which just adds more questions."

"Interesting. What happened after he ripped out your throat?"

"I turned to ashes. My whole body went ablaze with a pain I have never and hope to never feel again."

"You died?!" yelled Ash.

"Yes," I muttered, feeling a bit of guilt that I hadn't told him sooner.

"Interesting," said Yujin. "You are extremely rare indeed. I bet the vampire also burned up. Each scion is different in how they kill our kind."

"You know what I am? And who my parents are?" I asked excitedly.

"Oh, god no. There are too many that could be your godly parent. The Phoenix is represented through so many people."

"What?" I asked.

"Don't worry about it," Yujin laughed. "You can go

now."

"But…" I began.

Yujin just waved me off and made a fake yawn.

"Grandfather!" exclaimed Tessa.

A look from her caused her to back down and out the door.

"I told you this was a bad idea," said Ash. He just wants you to think he knows everything, but he doesn't know a single thing."

"I've told you all that you need to know. The ancestry doesn't matter as much as the type. And you are a rare one indeed, Rai Eckles. Ashlan Remus Ulfr, you are not strong enough to stand up to me and will never be so lower your hackles and take your bird with you."

Ash's tense body relaxed, and he grabbed my hand.

"We need to go," said Ash.

"Do send my progeny in after you leave," Yujin called out.

"I can wait for you," I whispered to Tessa as I passed her.

"No. Go home. If you antagonize him, you've already allowed him entry to your home. And going to a hotel won't work. We both know you don't have the money to find a new apartment," she said with a heavy sigh.

There was a fear in her eyes that I will never forget as she closed the door behind her.

Chapter Seventeen

I couldn't sleep that night. I was worried about Tessa. I should have been used to it by now, but she hadn't texted me back. A million things went through my head as to what happened, none of them were good. I sat over a cup of coffee at the dining room table as the sun rose, worn out but too many thoughts distracting me.

"You're awake already," Ash said groggily as he came into the kitchen.

"Huh? Oh, I haven't been asleep yet," I said with a stifled yawn.

Ash facepalmed and said, "You need to get to sleep. You won't be any good to anyone if you're too worn out."

"What if I got Tessa killed? She looked scared when she went in," I said, and laid my face in my hands.

"She would have run if she thought that was possible. I'm sure she was just being scolded for her pet standing up to him," Ash said as he looked through the fridge.

"Do you really think so?" I asked hopefully.

He grunted a yes. And while I didn't really believe it, I wanted to hope it was true. I made my way to my bed and lay there, much too tired to sleep. I don't know how long I lay there, but I had to have fallen asleep because I woke to the fading sunlight. Loud noises came from the living area, and I groaned and turned back over. I couldn't deal with werewolves right now. My door creaked open, and I turned to see Ash looking in on me.

"You're awake?" asked Ash, and he walked over.

"Barely. I'm gonna go back to bed. I'm not really in a people mood."

"When are you ever?" laughed Ash. "Sorry about the noise. I will try to keep them down, but I can't promise much."

"It's fine. Have fun and don't worry about me."

He sat on my bed and touched my shoulder, "Rai, if you need me, I can kick them all out."

"I'm fine. I promise."

"Okay," he said and softly brushed my cheek before he got up, "But if you need anything…"

"I know. I know."

It was still dark out when I sat up screaming. I had a dream that turned into a nightmare. I was on a picnic with Tessa, and everything was going nicely. If you discounted the sunny day, it would have felt real. I had been talking to her when she leaned in towards me. Then she changed into Pastor Thomas and ripped into my neck. The pain shot through me, and that was when I woke up.

Ash burst into my room and saw me breathing heavily as I sat in bed. He walked over to me, and I wrapped my arms around him and buried my face in his bare chest.

"Are you okay?" he asked and put a hand on my head.

"Just stay with me for the night," I said softly.

I scooted back and he got into the bed. I laid my head on his chest, and he wrapped an arm around me. The warmth of his body and the beating of his heart soothed me enough to fall back to sleep. When I woke up, I was the little spoon, and Ash was snoring softly. It was cute. It had been a while since we had slept in the same bed. Thinking back on it, it would have been around the time he would have started changing. In his arms, I felt a little guilty because the dreams I had were all of Tessa. I wanted to stay like that a little longer in that position, but the growling in my stomach wouldn't let me. I had slept all of yesterday away, so I couldn't remember the last time I had eaten. As I moved out from under his arm, he stirred.

"Up already?" he asked groggily.

"Already? I've slept an entire day away," I laughed and stood up.

"Oh right," he said with a yawn.

He got up, too, and made his way to his room to fall back asleep. I laughed at him and went to make myself some eggs and bacon. Ash woke up around noon, and since the sun was up, I expected not to hear from Tessa, so we went down to the beach.

"Are you going to try this time?" grinned Ash.

"You know what…sure. I'll try it," I said.

Ash stared at me dumbfounded before he did a toothy grin.

"Just once."

"That won't do anything you'll fall over. At least give me an hour of your time after all that cuddling," joked Ash.

My face turned red, and I just nodded in agreement. He took me by the hand and led me into the water. For the next hour, I spent most of my time face planting into the water, but it was fun. And Ash seemed to also enjoy himself as he tried to teach me.

"Yep, I tried. Not doing that again," I said, waterlogged as I crawled up to the beach and lay in the sand.

"You did fine. And I like you all wet," Ash said with a wink.

"Stooooop," I said and laughed as I threw sand at him.

BLOOD AND MOONLIGHT

As I dried off in the summer sun, Ash went back out to do his own surfing. For the first time, I paid little attention to Ash and watched the people around me. All these people just went about their life, not knowing about the other side. Or even worse, some of them were probably from the other side. How many people did I see every day and night were vampires or werewolves, or who knows what else? How many of these people were like me and didn't know it? Did all scions grow up abandoned and not knowing who they were?

I was lost in watching a couple playing with their young children when Ash came up to me as the sun set.

"That's not creepy at all. A grown person watching kids playing," Ash said, and lightly hit my leg with his foot.

"I'm not JUST watching the kids," I protested, "Just that normal life seems like it was forever ago. Now I can't help but wonder who is normal and who isn't."

"If it helps, they are normal," Ash said.

"It doesn't," I muttered.

He helped me up and made our way to get some funnel cake. I lost my appetite as I thought of how easily those people I had been watching could die. I had died, and nobody had been able to stop it from happening. How many people have died by people like Isiak and Corri? Or even from people like the werewolves that had attacked me, Tessa, and Beka. I hadn't even seen Beka since we had gotten back to town. I picked at my funnel cake and noticed that Ash looked at me worried.

"It's fine. I'm fine. I swear. Just a lot has happened these last few days," I said and gave a half smile.

He wanted to say something, but let it go as we made our way back home. Once home, I turned on a movie called The Good Guys. The beginning credits were just finishing when Ash tensed up seconds before a knock came at the door.

"I'll get it," I said and jumped up, knowing it had to be Tessa.

If it had been his friends, they would have barged right in. If it had been a normal person, he wouldn't have reacted. And if it had been a different vampire, he probably would have growled and been ready to fight.

I opened the door and Tessa stood there. Her hair was down, covering one eye, and she wore a black tank top with a black and red miniskirt.

"Hi," I said breathlessly.

She smiled at me, and I wrapped my arms around her in a bear hug. She hugged me back, but much softer.

"You're okay, come in," I said and smiled.

"I'm sorry I didn't come sooner," she said, coming in. "Hello, Wolfy."

"Hello," Ash said with a slight wave.

"Don't antagonize him," I sighed.

"It wasn't meant to be. Sorry, Ash."

"It's fine," Ash said.

"We're watching a movie. Want to watch it?" I asked.

"If I'm not intruding," she said.

"Nah, it'll be fun," I said.

I sat in the middle of them as Ash started the movie back up. As the movie went on, Tessa curled up into me with her arms wrapped round my arm and her head on my shoulder. Ash looked over and saw and rolled his eyes. He looked at his phone and got up.

"I got something I gotta deal with," said Ash, and he walked out.

"What's his issue?" Tessa asked as she watched him

leave.

"Don't worry about it," I said and laid my head on top of hers. "I was worried about you. What happened?"

"Nothing," she said quietly.

I scooted back to face her, and she looked down at the couch.

"Talk to me," I said and raised her face to mine.

I pushed her hair out of her face, and there was a large bruise on her covered eye.

"What happened?" I exclaimed.

"It's fine…"

I touched her face gently.

"I'm going to kill Yujin."

"You can't. Isiak was also the one who did it. It's not as bad as it looks. It will heal fast…"

"Why did he?"

"Great-great grandfather is… elevating my status. That is one reason I came over. To ask you to come to my ascension this weekend. I will be over Isiak. This was to show me that I will never be stronger than him no matter my status," explained Tessa.

I kissed her softly on the forehead, then said, "I wouldn't miss it for the world."

Chapter Eighteen

With a mischievous glint in her eyes, Tessa pushed me onto my back and straddled me. She held me down with playful force, and a seductive smile played across her navy lips.

"So, we're finally alone," she purred.

Her words dripped with seduction and sent shivers down my spine.

"Uh…" I said, very articulately.

Her lips brushed against mine, quick and gentle. As she pulled back, she gave me a toothy grin that sent my heart beating faster.

"The movie isn't over yet," I taunted her with a smirk of my own.

"Oh, so now we're watching a movie?" she teased, arching an eyebrow playfully.

"Unless you have something better in mind…" I trailed off, running a finger lightly up her arm.

"It just so happens that I do," she whispered, sending a shiver through me.

Her cold hands slipped under my shirt, and I couldn't help but whimper at the sensation. But instead of stopping, Tessa slid the shirt off me and kissed her way down my chest. I reached for her shirt, wanting to return the favor, but she pinned my wrists above my head.

"Not so fast," she breathed into my ear before she nipped at it gently.

BLOOD AND MOONLIGHT

My body burned for her touch as she straddled me and rubbed against me. A soft moan escaped my lips at the feeling of her pressed against me. She let out a soft moan in my ear and sent waves of desire through me. She kissed down my neck, her cold lips cooled the burning sensation on my skin. But at the same time, her touch ignited something deeper within me. With one hand still pinning mine above my head, she traced patterns on my inner thigh with the other.

"What if..." I started to say.

She cut off my words with a kiss that held a hunger that I matched as she unbuttoned my pants. Another moan escaped from me as her hand reached in and found its destination as she bit my lip. The thrill quickly vanished as I tasted blood in my mouth. I opened my eyes and saw Tessa as she stared at me with crimson eyes, a hunger inside them that I couldn't fathom.

"Stop..." I managed to gasp out, struggling against her hold on me.

But it was useless, as her fangs grew longer, and a wicked smile spread across her face. A sadistic glee shined in her eyes as she lowered her face toward my neck. Panic flooded through me as she sank her teeth into my neck. I tried to scream and fight against her, but no sound escaped from my paralyzed body.

Chapter Nineteen

I woke up with a jolt and looked around. Curled up on top of me was Tessa, her hair draped over my fully clothed chest. I touched my lip and felt nothing out of the ordinary.

"Do you usually moan out my name when you sleep?" She asked when she felt me moving, "Your heart was beating pretty fast. Want to share with the class what happened?"

"N... No," I stammered and turned red.

She laughed and kissed me on the nose.

"Ash came back. He's in his room. I better get going. Sun will be up in a few hours. It... was nice to see you," she said.

"Come over anytime," I said and ran my fingers through her hair.

She closed her eyes and sighed contently.

"Stop, or I might stay. And neither of us want to see me getting a tan," she breathed.

A quick kiss on the lips, and she was gone, and I was on the couch alone. I closed my eyes and saw her face again, but from my dream, and opened them quickly. I wasn't going to get back to sleep anytime soon. Instead, I decided to make an early breakfast. Maybe it would also wake Ash up and draw him out of his room. It was late morning when Ash finally woke up.

"Morning," I said chipperly.

He didn't even look my way as he grabbed a banana and headed out the door. I jumped off the couch and followed him.

"Ash?" I was concerned.

He ignored me and finished his banana in two bites. He threw the peel in the trash at the apartment building's entrance and still hadn't so much as looked at me. I tried to get in front of him, but he just walked around me without looking down. After the second time, he stretched his legs before he took off running. I didn't even try to keep up. He was like a bolt of lightning when he wanted to be. I went back upstairs to finish the show I had been watching when he had woken up. Great, Ash was mad at me about something, and I couldn't close my eyes without seeing Tessa trying to kill me. The day could not get any worse.

I decided to try and take a walk to clear my head. The bright sun and some exercise could help. I had no destination in mind, I just wanted to enjoy the heat on my skin as I walked, earbuds in with My First Story blaring. I ended up at a secluded part of the beach, where me and Ash usually went, but he wasn't there. I did see a figure climb up the rocky cliffside, though, and that caused me to pause and take out my earbuds. It wouldn't have been too hard to climb; it was an outcropping, and rocks spiked out at different angles, but it was wet. The ocean always pelted it on a wavy day, and it had to have been covered in algae. The person walked towards me with an air of confidence in a long leather jacket that hid their whole body, and a hood pulled up over their head that obscured any features. Something inside told me that wasn't right. It had to be almost a hundred and ten degrees out. I would have been dying in that just standing still, and they had climbed up a rock face and didn't seem the least bit exhausted. My curiosity got the better of me, though, as I stood there and watched them approach.

They walked past me, and the air seemed to drop thirty degrees. I shivered with the sudden drop in temperature and rubbed my arms to warm up. I was grabbed from behind and thrown to the ground with enough force to knock the wind out of me. Under the hood, I saw their jaws unhinged like a snake, and their lower and upper canines grew longer. A forked tongue snaked out and lapped at my face as I squirmed.

"You smell so sweet," came an unearthly voice, "Maybe I will allow myself a small taste."

"Get off, you can't eat me if you want to live," I groaned and pushed against the creature on me.

Even with all my strength, I couldn't budge them even an inch. A sharp pain in my side made me cry out as my arms dropped to my side. They brought a long bowie knife up that dripped with blood. The blood dripped on my face, and the forked tongue flicked out and licked the knife clean. A small moan escaped its lips. My eyes grew wide as I realized what had happened. Another stab slid between my ribs and pierced my heart, and the fire inside me flooded through me once again. I knew I wasn't meant to be experiencing anything. The creature looked down at me, a satisfied smile on its face.

"Cazimir sends his deepest regards Scion. Another one gone from this world. This time Yujin won't try to find us. So sad that we must let that blood go to waste," said the creature.

I heard them walk off, but I couldn't move my body or my eyes. They had to have been glossed over, with that glassy look in dead bodies, but my soul still looked out. I couldn't even cry out as the fire burned through me, starting from the heart and spreading out through my veins. In a flash fire, I lay naked on the beach in the middle of the day. Luckily for me, my phone had fallen out of my pocket and lay in the sand a few feet away. It took all the energy I had to drag myself to a cropping of rocks that blocked me from sight if people walked by after I grabbed my phone.

"Ash… I need you," I said softly to the voicemail I had been sent too, "I'm at our place."

It was the most I could do before I passed out from the energy loss. I woke up to the sounds of voices and was in my bed. The sun was down, and I was in Ash's oversized sweatpants.

"Leave," Ash growled.

"What happened?" Tessa said, anger in her voice, "Why won't you let me see him?"

"His life was fine until you showed up. Now, he's nearly died more times than I care to count. How do I know you aren't responsible for it?"

"What would I have to gain from doing that? Especially when there is a werewolf always near him," Tessa's voice rose. "I would be putting myself at risk if I made any mistake."

"You might not have anything to gain, but that uncle or grandfather of yours would. And from what I know of vampires, they can easily bend the weaker ones to their will."

"You. Are. An. Idiot. If that was the case, then turning a vampire wouldn't cause so many issues. It's true that the older you are, the more powerful you can be, but we can't compel each other. All the things you think you know are from the darker brethren. IF you'd just listen to me for once."

There was the sound of something heavy hitting the wall outside my room, and another lighter sound of the opposite wall being hit by something. I stumbled out of bed and opened my door. Ash was in his Teen Wolf form with a hand around Tessa's throat. He held her off the floor and at eye level against the wall. Her eyes were red, her teeth bared, and her nails dug into his outstretched arm. To the side of me, the couch laid where thrown, below a crack along the wall.

"Stop," I said raspily.

They didn't hear me, and Ash yelped as blood flew from his forearm. He dropped Tessa, and she moved away from him as she circled.

"Stop!" I yelled and then coughed.

They turned around and Ash returned to human form.

"You're awake," Tessa said and jumped on me.

I stumbled and fell onto my back. Ash lifted Tessa off me by the collar and put her on her feet to his side.

"Are you okay?" he asked worriedly.

"You saved me," I said and wrapped my arms around him.

"You called…" he said, and I felt his body get hotter.

I let go and smiled up at him before I turned to Tessa. "Ash is going to hate this, but I need to go see Yujin."

"What?" exclaimed Ash.

I pointed to him with an 'I told you so' face.

"He's not here. He won't be back until my ascension."

Ash looked down at her and said, "I knew it. You are using him for power."

"I am not!" growled Tessa.

I facepalmed, "I don't care who is or isn't doing what. I died. And it was not as pleasant as the last one. I was… trapped in my dead body as the thing that killed me talked."

I explained to them what I had seen, and watched the horror on Tessa's face when I described the features of the creature.

"How did my darker kin make their way in the sun?" she whispered.

"That was a vampire?" I asked.

"Sort of. Something happened to them, and while they seem like us, we are vastly different. They have the religious weakness if a true believer wields it, and the older ones can compel the younger ones. Some have esoteric abilities. They can do the mist and animal shifting too. Basically, if you think of Dracula, it is them," she said.

"They mentioned they had to kill me the way they did because Yujin would try to find them otherwise. That is why I need to talk to him. And that Cazimir sends his regards."

"I've never heard of anyone named Cazimir," Tess said with crossed arms and a thoughtful look on her face.

I heard Ash audibly gasp at the name.

"Do you know something, Ash?" I asked.

"No. It can't be, anyway. That name is too old for it to matter," Ash said with a shake of his head.

"We are talking about vampires. I don't think age matters," I sighed.

"He wasn't a vampire. That is the name of one of the first wolves. So, it has to be one of those creatures using his name," said Ash with clear disgust on his face.

"No use dwelling on it. They think I'm dead, so I should be fine now. I hope. We just have to wait a few days and be safe," I said.

"I'm not leaving your side," said Tessa.

"You are not staying here," said Ash.

"I am not leaving. WE need to make sure he stays

safe," said Tessa.

"No."

"Yes."

"One day. Please. One day without this fighting. She can stay," I said. "Though, you might be more safe at home if something does come."

"Isiak will be happy I'm gone for a while. I just need to create a place where I can sleep in the day," said Tessa.

"My room will work. It's got the one window, but we can buy some paint to black it out if we need to," I said.

Ash's face grew red with anger, but he said nothing.

Chapter Twenty

The night went by a lot more awkwardly than I had thought. Ash never came out of his room, which left me and Tessa alone. Which would have been fine, but me and Tessa alone were one of the reasons I was sure Ash was mad at me. On top of that, after the dream and what happened earlier, I couldn't stop thinking that she was going to be the one to kill me for a third time. I turned on a random movie that was just on TV. I knew it was a stupid thought, but she knew something was wrong.

"Why are you avoiding me?" Tessa asked halfway through the movie, and we were on separate ends of the couch.

"I'm not," I lied.

She just looked at me and frowned.

"You're going to call me dumb…"

"I already think you're dumb. Is it Ash? Does he… are you…?" she asked.

"Wow, thanks. It's more than just him. Me and him are… I don't know. What are me and you?" I asked.

She scooted closer, "You tell me what we are."

She saw me flinch and backed up.

"Sorry," I sighed, "The other night… I had a dream and… you killed me."

"I would never!" she yelled appalled.

"I know! But it was so vivid. You were on top of me, and then… when I woke up, you were on top of me."

97

She threw a cushion at me, "Is that why you moaned my name? Cause I was killing you? Why didn't you talk to me about it?"

"Well, it didn't start out that way," I pouted.

"What way did it..." Tessa began, "Oh."

She turned red and looked away.

"Shush," I said as I felt my face getting red too.

"Well don't expect that to happen any time soon now," she muttered.

"What? No. I didn't..."

She giggled and laid her feet across my lap as she lay down. I pouted at her, and it just made her laugh louder.

"I do like you. It's why I am here. I plan to stay here until you realize that you want to be with me," she said, almost too quiet for me to hear.

I rubbed her legs absently. I wanted to feel her cold lips against mine, but at the same time I wouldn't mind feeling Ash's also. I had thought about Ash since I had come to understand what those types of feelings were. And the only time he had kissed me was to try and make sure I didn't go with Tessa. But I ached to do it again, almost as much as I ached for Tessa. She laughed and kicked at my hand, and I realized my hands had absent-mindedly started rubbing her feet.

"Sorry," I said and lifted my hands up.

"It's fine, I'm just ticklish there," she said and smiled at me.

The night before her ascension, Tessa returned home to get everything ready. Leaving me and Ash alone for the first time in three nights. He was in his room when she left, and I knocked on the door.

"What?" he asked.

"Can we talk?" I asked.

"Isn't that what we're doing?"

I rolled my eyes, "You know what I mean."

"What do we have to talk about?"

"Us."

He opened his door and leaned against the door frame. His shirtless body brought a longing to me.

"What about us?" he asked.

"I don't want you mad at me."

"What, possibly, could I be mad about?" Ash said sarcastically.

"You saw me and Tessa cuddled up. After that, you've been distant. And a lot angrier at her in a different way than you had been."

He looked away.

I reached out and touched his abs.

"Stop," he said softly.

"I need you to know that I've always liked you. You were the only one for the longest time. I didn't care that you were popular or that I had nobody else around. Then I met Tessa and it got complicated. She's... different. We connect in a unique way. Like me, she had nobody. I can relate to her. And she might have started out shy, but she shows her affection," I said as I moved closer. "While you keep an exterior up. I don't know what to think. I don't know what you want."

He grabbed me roughly and pulled me into a passionate kiss, his lips crushing mine with an urgent need. I could feel the heat radiating from him, it consumed me with desire.

"Does that answer anything?" he asked breathlessly as he pulled back for air.

My mind was swirling with emotions, and I needed more.

"I'm not sure," I said teasingly, my heart racing with anticipation. "I think I need to hear it again."

With a wicked grin, he dragged me into his room and threw me onto his bed as if I weighed nothing. As he climbed on top of me, I ran my hands over his chiseled chest, feeling the hard muscles ripple beneath my touch. He claimed my lips again, his tongue exploring every inch of my mouth as our fingers intertwined in a desperate tangle. His lips trailed down to my neck, sending electric shocks through my body as he nipped and sucked at my skin. I couldn't help but gasp, my body arching into his as the pleasure consumed me. His smirk sent shivers down my spine, knowing he had complete control over me.

As our bodies moved together in perfect harmony, he brought my hand up to his chest and pressed it against his pounding heart.

"My body will keep you warm," he growled hungrily, "and my heart beats in exhilaration because of you."

His words ignited a fire within me, knowing that he wanted me just as much as I wanted him.

"She doesn't have a heart to beat for you," he added possessively.

I groaned and crawled out from under him, "You know... I think you're the one who needs to decide how they really feel. Don't take this the wrong way, but I think you're just being territorial over me. Can't say I'm a fan. You were all I had for so long. She comes along, and suddenly you're burning for me? Find out why you really hate her, then we can talk."

I slammed his door behind me and went to my room,

full of pent-up sexual tension that was not going to have a fulfilling release. I didn't talk to Ash the next day, and not just because he spent most of it avoiding me. He would see me, and his face would go red, and he'd hurry back to his room. I was getting ready to go to see Tessa as the sun set when a knock came at the door.

"We don't want any!" I yelled.

The knock came more insistent, and Ash came out of his room as I checked the peephole. Rafael stood in the hall, stooped and liver-spotted as ever.

I opened the door, "Good evening."

"Good evening, Master Eckles. I am to bring you to my Master."

"I was just about to head over. I don't need a limo," I groaned.

"We are not headed to the mansion. He wishes to see you in a different location."

Ash turned to return to his room.

"Master Ulfr, you have been requested to come also," piped up Rafael.

"If I don't want to?" Ash said as he turned around.

"Then you risk angering an incredibly old vampire who knows, and has been invited into, where you live. Maybe he won't take the slight as anything. But, who knows the whims of an ancient," Rafael said and headed down the hall.

Ash sighed, "I'll get ready quickly."

I waited for him and we walked down together. Beka was there and held the door open. My senses started to tingle. I was worried something had happened to Tessa. Otherwise, she would have been the one to get me. I saw Ash tense up.

"Hey, Beka," I said as I came up to her.

She just nodded at me as I got in behind Rafael. Ash

got in behind me. Sitting on the other side of the back was Tessa.

"What's going on?" I asked.

Tessa shrugged, "I wish I knew. I woke up and was told by Beka to get into the limo."

"All will be explained in time," said Rafael as we started to move.

I sat next to Tessa, "Any clue if this is normal?"

"I don't know. This has never happened before," she said.

Ash came over, "Why am I here? I don't need to be here."

"Again, I don't know anything. Great-great-grandfather is the only one who has the answers."

The drive took an hour, and at one point turned down a very bumpy dirt road. As I looked out the window, I realized we were driving through a forest. When we stopped, it was in front of a large cavern entrance.

"This way, please. Stay close if you cannot see in the dark," Rafael said as he opened the door.

He opened the trunk after we were all out and pulled out a battery-powered lantern. Beka and I stayed close to Rafael in the front, while Tessa and Ash walked behind when we entered the cavern. They were both tense, and it made me feel we were going to be ambushed. Through twists and turns, I began to hate that vampires seemed to like mazes. Probably so their prey couldn't flee, but who knew? Eventually, we came to a chamber that was too dark to see the other side with the light from the lantern. Tessa and Ash stood on either side of me. Tessa grabbed me by the hand, and Ash put a hand on my shoulder. Rafael walked forward with Beka in tow and lit a large fire. The chamber lit up and the smoke rose out of a natural hole in the ceiling.

"This doesn't make sense," whispered Ash. "Why did they lead us here?"

"Get ready to run wolfy. I don't like this," whispered Tessa.

As I looked around, there were so many people on raised levels of the chamber. Sitting next to Isiak and Corri were two people I never expected to see. Ash's parents stared down at us. His fingers dug into my shoulder, and it made me realize he had seen them, too. A small shake of his father's head caused the grip to loosen.

"I'm not running," Ash growled lowly. "Why are my parents here?"

"What?" Tessa said and searched the crowd.

"The two beside your aunt and uncle," said Ash.

"It's worse," said Tessa. "There are not just vampires in this chamber. It's split between werewolves and vampires."

"It's my pack from back home," said Ash.

"And my whole family," mumbled Tessa.

I searched the crowd, "Where is Yujin?"

"All will be explained," Rafael said. "Now follow me."

He put the three of us on different sides of a circular indent in the ground. It was almost twenty feet across at each point. I was put on the southern end, while Ash and Tessa were put on the eastern and western ends. The indent went down at an angle until it was about seven feet down at the center, where Beka made her way to.

"Let this ascension begin," bellowed out Yujin as he appeared at the northern tip of the circle.

Almost everyone cheered loudly. Isiak, Corri, Ulric, and Lyra were the only ones in the raised areas who showed no emotion.

"I have gathered everyone here today because we need to come together. Something bigger than a petty squabble between us creatures of the night," boomed Yujin's voice. "Here we have a Scion, Werewolf, and Vampire, all being friends. If our youngest generation can do so, then we can do the same for a brief moment in time."

Ash and Tessa looked at each other in recognition of what was about to happen. It looked like they tried to move, but they just shuffled in place. I tried to speak, but my mouth wouldn't move.

"Things from the darker depths have risen. Scions who befriend one side die, then the other side gets the blame, and we continue a war being blamed for things we have never done," continued Yujin. "But, with this ascension, we will all work together to find these darker brethren from both sides."

Yujin walked around the circle and put a circle of blood on each of our heads, "Usually an ascension has a binding, a marriage if you will, between two vampires from different clans. This time, it will be a binding between three different clans. Isiak Lister, the legal guardian of Theresa Belle Wentzel, do you agree to this?"

Though his eyes burned with anger, Isiak stood and said, "As the legal guardian of Tessa, I give my consent for this binding."

"Ulric Ulysses Ulfr, as the patriarch for Ashlan Remus Ulfr, do you agree to this?" bellowed Yujin.

Ulric stood next to Isiak, his eyes filled with anger. "As father to Ash, I, too, give my consent to this binding."

"And as I am the oldest in this area, I, Yujin, give my consent to this binding of Ashlan Ulfr and Theresa Wentzel, along with their binding to Rai Eckles."

The cheers went up again, and I realized that I was

now, in the eyes of these clans, married to Tessa and Ash.

"Now that the precursor is out of the way," said Yujin as he made his way back to the northern part of the circle, "A good ascension starts with a sacrifice."

As he looked at me, a smile spread across his lips, then I heard Beka wail. I looked down, and Beka writhed in pain on the ground. Tessa let out a shrill shriek and struggled against whatever bound them to the spot. Ash shifted from human to wolf to hybrid form as he tried to break free, but nothing worked. I jumped down into the pit, ignoring the pain in my leg as it twisted, and grabbed Beka. I tried to hold her down to keep her from writhing, but her wailing got even louder.

"What's wrong?" I asked. "I can't help if I don't know what's wrong."

Yujin wrenched me from Beka and held me back.

"Stop this. Please," I begged.

Before I could end the word, Beka dispersed into a fine mist. It flew up and began to circle overhead. The sounds of Beka's wails reached a crescendo as it spun, then it exploded out. As I looked up from the hole, half of it absorbed into Ash and the other half into Tessa. The cheering seemed to shake the cave as my world spun around. Anger burned inside me, and fire engulfed my body. Yujin sped away from me, his hand blackened from the flames. I flew out of the hole twenty feet up, surrounded in flames that were in the shape of a falcon, with the wings spread out wide.

Then the fire went out, and as darkness overtook me, I saw Ash holding a sobbing Tessa as they knelt over my body. I crashed into my body and gasped awake.

"It's okay," I rasped and reached out to touch them both.

Chapter Twenty-One

"She's gone," Tessa bawled and wrapped her arms around me.

I stared at her and Ash as he rubbed her back.

"What exactly happened? What happened to Beka?" I asked.

"She was used as a sacrifice to make us stronger and tie us together. Magic doesn't work on you, so she didn't flow into you to connect your mind to ours," explained Ash. "The backlash of Tessa's pain flowed into me. I felt everything she did at that moment. Then you exploded into flames, but your body didn't turn to ashes, and she thought something had gone very, very wrong."

"We are leaving. Now," I snarled.

"I'm not sure we can. There is… more to this ritual. My becoming alpha and her becoming the matriarch of her family is not yet complete. Yujin is too ancient for me to risk the lives of my parents on."

I lifted Tessa as she sobbed into the crook of my neck and walked out of the hole side by side with Ash. Yujin stood there and glared at me. He hid his hand inside his cape, and a glimpse of it told me it was still burnt.

"Can we continue? It is almost over. This is beyond your meager understanding," Yujin said as he motioned to the side.

"If I just leave?" I said quietly.

"We have no need of you scion. The magic here does

not bind you. But you do get the offer of protection against the things that hunt your kind," said Yujin, "and I believe there are things you wish to discuss with me. Those are the reasons we are all gathered here."

"Cazimir," I said breathlessly.

"Oh, that is a name I have not heard in eons. Something even I have tried to avoid," Yujin scowled.

Tessa leapt out of my arms at Yujin, but Ash caught her by the arm.

He pulled her against him and held her as he whispered, "Not now. You will just die."

I stared at them in shock.

"The magic," Yujin explained.

"It's controlling how they think? Stop it now," I growled.

"Not how they think. It has made their minds intertwined. To feel how the other feels. To not view each other as rivals but as one and the same."

"It's fine," Ash said softly. "It isn't so bad."

"I will never forgive you," Tessa snarled as her eyes pulsed a deep purple.

Yujin waved her threat off, "There is only one more thing you need to do. To accept this yourself. Drink from the sacred fountain and merge hearts as well as minds. For the first time since the dawn of man, the Lycan and Vampir, together as one. Even if it is only the House of Blood and the Pack of the Radiant Moonlight."

He led the three of us to a naturally formed pillar that formed into the shape of a bowl at the tip. Inside the bowl was a strange milky liquid.

"Now drink of the liquid and be bound to each other until death," said Yujin.

I scooped up some with my hand and drank it. As I did, I felt and tasted nothing. It was almost like drinking air. Tessa came up next, took a sip, and seemed to glow. As Ash took his sip and began to glow, the light shot out of them and seemed to flow into the other until it faded. Ash walked over to Tessa, tipped her head up, leaned over, and kissed her. My eyes widened in shock and my heart raced in jealousy, but I wasn't sure if it was because she was being kissed or because he was kissing someone else. Before I could even think of it, he stood over me and kissed me with more intensity than he had her. I returned the kiss with the same intensity, but it was over much too quickly. When he moved away, Tessa stared at me with a small smile on her face and took me by the hand.

"Things have happened, and this will be the worst day of my life, while also being the best. Rai Eckles, no matter what happens, me and you are together in life and death. Even if it comes with your loyal dog as a bonus," Tessa said, the sadness still evident in her voice even as she joked.

Before I could respond, she pulled me into a long, deep kiss. I wrapped my arms around her, the feel of her body against mine just felt right to me. Yujin and Ash both cleared their throats and we parted.

"Now, we are done," said Yujin. "Meet me at my room later tonight."

"Can I see my parents?" Ash asked.

"Best wait until they come to see you. You are their alpha now after all. No weakness should be shown in front of the pack," said Yujin.

Tessa glared at him, "What is to stop Isiak from trying to kill me?"

"My little Tessa, your own power of course. Beka was the only sacrifice that could make you strong enough not to die to Isiak," explained Yujin. "Well, Rai would have worked also, but that would not work out to my own plans. She has known you since you turned, almost a decade. She is the closest person to you and a reminder of your dead father. That connection boosts the power of the ritual. Since you have decided to forgo any other connections in this life, until you met your new husband here, I had to get creative to protect you from my progeny."

Tessa grabbed me and Ash by the hand and pulled us away.

"Don't forget to come visit," Yujin sang out as we left.

Chapter Twenty-Two

The three of us sat on the couch back at the apartment. Ash sat with his arm across the back of the couch. I was in the middle, and Tessa had her feet curled to the side as she laid her head on my shoulder.

"Are you two okay?" I asked.

"I'm fine," said Ash.

"Given what has happened, I could be worse," said Tessa.

"I think I should go see Yujin alone."

"No!" they said simultaneously.

"He's already done so much to you two. He can't do anything to me."

"Except kill you without you being able to react," said Ash.

"Won't be the first time."

"You are not leaving me ever again," said Tessa firmly.

"And I have to make sure you both stay out of trouble," Ash said as he ruffled my hair.

"Fine," I agreed. "We better get ready."

As I got up, a knock came at the door.

"Rafael, again?" I asked.

"No," said Ash. "You two go on ahead, I will catch up."

He opened the door and his parents stood there.

"Hi stepparents," I joked, since they had always felt like a second set of parents to me anyway.

They didn't smile back; they just looked at me angrily. I scooted by them and mouthed sorry back to Ash. Tessa kissed Ash on the cheek as she went by. It still was a bit weird to me, but I could see myself getting used to it quick enough. It was a short walk through the warm night. Me and Tessa walked hand in hand as we came to the gated community, then through to the large mansion in the back. As we walked in, Jarret was there.

"Oh, the princess has returned," Jarret said sarcastically.

Tessa glared at him, and her eyes grew a deep purple. He sped away, and her eyes turned back to normal.

"Why do your eyes turn that color now?" I asked. "And what did you do to him?"

"What color? And I didn't do anything to him except scare him."

"Your eyes become purple now, not red."

"That's... strange. I have never heard of someone with purple."

"Guess you're even more special than I originally thought," I joked and playfully bumped into her as we made our way to Yujin's room.

As we neared, the door opened before we were close. Rafael stood on the other side and came out and ushered us inside without a word. For the first time, Yujin looked tired.

"Nice of you to join me," Yujin said, his voice weak. "Where is Ulfr?"

His hand was wrapped in bandages.

"His parents dropped by. Can we finally talk?" I asked.

Tessa went over to him, her face filled with worry, "You look terrible. What happened?"

His eyes flashed to me, "Nothing you need to worry about. Let us discuss what has happened."

Rafael brought in two chairs, and we sat down.

"So, where did you hear that name?" Yujin asked as Rafael left again.

"Cazimir? I was told that he sent his regards after I was killed by some creatures. They could unhinge their jaws and drink my blood without dying. But they didn't know about my ability," I explained.

"Your kind is the rarest of them all. In all my experiments with scions, I had never encountered one who could not die," said Yujin. "Let us talk of Cazimir, the great beast."

"Who is he?" I asked.

"Oh, he was great. A creature that prowled the lands of what you call Pangea. He was one of the first things created from the darkness, alongside the first of the vampires. When humans began to evolve, so primitive and stupid, he saw himself as their protector. He was viewed as their own personal god. The thing that protected them from the giant bats in the sky," said Yujin. "You see we had been bats during this time. As humans evolved, so did we. Some evolved into the vampire bats you see today, losing all sense of their own selves. The rest turned into what we are. Our ability to turn others comes from the need to stay alive as we were hunted like rabid animals. So, we learned to blend in and take what we wanted."

"There is no way this is the same Cazimir," said Tessa. "Werewolves would know of him."

"It is not so simple. While it is true we evolved how we did, and the werewolves became how you know them, they did not come from Cazimir directly," explained Yujin.

"Cazimir was not the only one. He had a whole pack. Some of those stayed with Cazimir. The rest mingled in with the Homo Sapiens who began to emerge. The werewolf trait is passed down by blood and cannot be given like the vampire trait can be. That offshoot who left Cazimir is what created the modern werewolves. They passed down the stories of his greatness."

"What he became afterwards was never uttered. He grew filled with rage at being betrayed and left by his pack, and his path led him to our darker brethren. The ones who would not give up their ways to fit in with the humans to survive. The cursed ones took that pack in. How they did it, I will never know, but they created hybrids. So, Cazimir is most definitely still alive. Half vampire, half werewolf," continued Yujin. "From the things you have said about them being able to taste your blood, it explains other things I have been confused about. Scions dying with bite marks. Both vampiric and wolf bites have been the causes. The number of scions have dwindled, even more since the time I used them to learn more about them. Somehow, our dark kin have evolved to be able to stand this blood. Interesting times indeed."

"There is no way any of that is possible," Tessa said, shocked.

"Have you met him?" I asked.

"Oh, it is very much possible. I met him. I fought him back in those dark ages," laughed Yujin.

"None of that is possible," Ash said as he came up behind us.

I jumped out of my chair and ran to him, "You're here."

He just grunted at me and stared at Yujin.

"Do not try to tell me what is possible. I have been

around since your people were fish in the ocean," Yujin said a bit of the fire returning to his voice.

"You are too weak right now, and I'm angry, so calm your voice," Ash said steely.

I thought Yujin was going to attack, but his body just sagged into itself.

"Back then the wolves and the bats kept to themselves, but I was more curious than my darker brethren. I wanted to know these things that roamed the ground while we roamed the air. That was when I met Cazimir. I learned fear that day. My brethren called me weak when I ran back to them, wings torn asunder by that wolf. That called me a fool for trying to get so close to the territory of the wolf and shunned me. That is the only reason I survived. When the first scion came, that helped what you call Australopithecus change to what you are now, the Homo genus, that started my change also. I evolved along with them, from bat to man. My Darker brethren created Australopithecus vampires that continued on to change Homo genus when they came about. Those, my sweet Tessa, are your ancestors. All dead now, unfortunately," said Yujin, a bit of sadness creeping into his weak voice.

"You are not?" asked Tessa, as confused as the rest.

"Not in any real sense. I've not turned anyone. The scion sided with the wolves, and my brethren wanted to destroy what that scion had caused to happen. If they could have, they would have wiped out humanity before it started," said Yujin. "That is also where the split in that first pack came about. Cazimir wanted to be the outside protectors. One who was worshipped and feared. Others felt that mixing in with them would let them protect themselves. And so, the werewolves and the vampires mixed with the species and evolved with them. Their war also kept the pool small and the normal humans safe from becoming anything but normal.

"In that anger for humans, and my brethren not wanting to change themselves, they become something darker. That still lived in the shadows. I've spent these eons tracking down my brethren and ending them. But a couple eluded me for a while. They created the cursed darker kin of modern vampires before I could wipe them out. That fear Cazimir had put into me in our first meeting has kept me running from him. And building my own family by joining with a matriarch or patriarch of that family. And when I have enough power in the family, taking over full control. To see that he is the one I have been searching for, the one killing all the scions that roam. Destiny likes to play games."

"Why are you so weak right now? Did something happen?" I asked.

"You know very well what happened," glared Yujin.

"My fire did that?!"

"It has sapped my energy," Yujin said as he held up a blackened hand, "It heals, but too slowly. The power of a sun god's flames it would seem. Now, I need to feast. I am starving and all three of you are starting to look like meals. I do not wish to die, and the other two would give me no nourishment, so please leave."

"Sun god?!" I exclaimed.

"You are a Phoenix. They are usually associated with the sun," Tessa said and pulled me out of the room. "You are always so hot to the touch that it even warms me up."

Ash followed behind us, his face told me he was lost in thought.

Chapter Twenty-Three

"So, are we safe here from these things that can drink me?" I asked as we entered the apartment.

"You should be. Even I couldn't enter this place when we first met," shrugged Tessa.

"That's if what we know is true. This thing, using the name Cazimir, has used zombies! Who knows what else they could use," said Ash.

"I need to get rest. I can feel the pull of slumber coming as the sunrise gets closer," said Tessa as she made her way to my room.

"We all need to get some rest after this long night," I said to Ash.

"I'm fine. I will stay awake to make sure nothing happens," Ash said and sat at the kitchen table.

"Are you sure?"

"Yes. You will need to get rest, so when you wake up, I can sleep. You can be the bridge between the day and night watches."

"That's what I have always wanted to be when I grew up. To be a bridge between day and night," I rolled my eyes.

"Hey, you're the one who decided to be a Phoenix, love. I don't make the rules," smirked Ash.

"This stuff isn't for the birds, if you ask me," I stuck out my tongue and made my way to my room.

I walked in as Tessa was removing her shirt.

"Uh..." I said quickly and turned around.

116

"Oh, I didn't realize you were coming," Tessa said and covered herself.

"Ash told me to get rest also," I said, my face ablaze.

She wrapped her arms around my waist and pressed her body against my back, "Well, there's still an hour until sunrise."

Her whisper sent a thrill up my body. After a moment, she shut the door and tugged at the hem of my shirt. I turned around and saw her naked back as she led me to the bed. My whole body had turned red, and I looked down, then up at the ceiling. She let go of my hand at the edge of the bed.

"You can look, you know," she said.

I looked down slowly and she laid there on the bed with one arm that propped up her head. The white sheet draped over her chest and ran between her legs. With her free hand she pointed her finger at me, then motioned with it to come.

"Is this the…" I started.

"Shh, don't talk. This may be all we get," she said softly.

She got to her knees and let the covers fall to the bed. I pinched my arm as I stared into her eyes, the pain making me still unsure if I was dreaming again or not.

"This is real," she purred as she ran her fingers under my shirt.

"Are you sure?" I shuddered.

"As sure as I am about how much I care about you," she said and lifted my shirt off.

I pushed her back onto the bed and she giggled as she threw my shirt to the side. I kissed slowly up her leg, and I heard soft murmurs from her as her hands found their way to my hair. The slower I kissed the more she pulled at my head to make me go faster. As I kissed her thigh and gently bit it, she gasped out a moan and pulled me up to her. She kissed me as her fingernails dug into my back, my hand roamed her thighs, the other keeping my weight off her as I hungrily devoured her lips and she moaned into my mouth, our tongues mingling in an intimate dance.

Her hips began to undulate, her passion rippling through her body as she arched into my touch. My heart pounded in time, with the raging tide of desire coursing through my veins. As our kiss deepened, I slowly inched my hand even higher, her skin cold and trembling. She quivered beneath me, her breaths coming out in hushed panting whispers. My fingers delicately traced the curve of her waist, then dipped lower, grazing the sensitive skin above her apex. With a sharp intake of breath, she thrust herself forward, her nails digging deeper into my back. I groaned half in pain, half in pleasure as she clawed down my back and started to undo my pants. Our breaths grew shallower and quicker, the air between us filled with anticipation. The heat and cold between our bodies became an almost palpable entity of its own.

The fire ignited within me, and our eyes locked with a bright passion. The world around me faded as I looked into her soul, my finger tracing itself lower as she pulled down my pants. The taste of her kiss was sweeter and more intoxicating than ever before. My breath hitched in my throat when she pressed herself against me; my body was on fire from head to toe, all sensation fading away except for the feeling of her hand moving up my thighs. Her lips parted and her tongue slid along my neck, making me shiver with delight.

"Please," she whispered into my ear breathlessly, "take me. Be mine now and forever."

"Forever," I moaned softly in response.

The following hour was a mix of ecstasy and pain, all a blur in my mind. She was careful not to break my skin as she bit into the nape of my neck to muffle her moans. As the night grew to an end, we laid naked, our bodies intertwined with each other and the covers. Her leg draped over my lower torso, the ice of her body cooled me off. Her head nestled gently on my chest as my finger traced lazy circles along her upper back, her breathing slowed until it ceased as she fell asleep.

"I love you," I murmured and kissed the top of her head, before falling off into a deep slumber.

I was nudged awake by a large hand. I had my face buried in the nape of Tessa's neck as I held her from behind. The smell of her stirred the lust inside me again, so that I forgot I had been nudged awake. Another, harder nudge made me turn. Ash stood over me, and the lust I had for Tessa welled up inside now for him.

"I need to get to sleep dude," Ash said groggily.

That brought me to my senses. I got out of the bed and put on a shirt and some sweatpants as Ash looked me up and down with a sly grin on his face.

"Yea, yea," I blushed and looked at the still form of Tessa.

I covered her up and followed Ash to his bedroom door. I ran my hand up his body and to his face.

"Get some good rest. I'll make sure I keep you both safe this time," I grinned and kissed him deeply.

He pulled me against his body, our tongues intertwining before he pulled back.

"Oh, I think I will have a great time sleeping now," rumbled Ash as he shut his door.

119

The sun had a few hours of life left, but I eagerly began to prepare dinner for Tessa. The weight of the past few days, filled with talk of vampires and werewolves, scions, and ancient beings, lifted from my mind as I immersed myself in one of my greatest passions - cooking. With flour dusting my cheeks and a determined gleam in my eye, I carefully measured out the ingredients for homemade spaghetti noodles. My grandmother's cherished recipe was ingrained in my mind, but I kept the worn index card nearby as I worked. Flour, eggs, olive oil, a pinch of salt - simple components that when combined, created noodles far superior to any store-bought variety.

As I kneaded the dough in the cramped kitchen, I could feel its stubborn resistance beneath my palms. But with patience and strength, it gradually yielded to me, transforming into a smooth, golden orb. With each roll of the rolling pin, the aroma of fresh bread filled the air. The dough thinned under my skilled hands until it reached the perfect thickness for cutting into delicate strands. I hung the noodles on a makeshift laundry line to dry as I turned my attention to the sauce. A generous glug of olive oil sizzled in the pot, before adding diced onions and minced garlic. Their sweet fragrances mingled together and filled the room as they softened over the heat. With precise movements, I crushed canned tomatoes and added them to the pot, their vibrant red color bursting with summertime energy.

The symphony of flavors continued to build as I added crushed tomatoes and a dollop of tomato paste to create a rich, layered base. Oregano and basil, dried but still potent, were sprinkled in along with a pinch of salt and pepper. To add some heat to the melody, I carefully added a dash of red pepper flakes. As the sauce simmered on the stovetop I stirred and tasted, fine-tuning the flavors with a splash of salt, a hint of sugar to balance the acidity, and a final flourish of freshly chopped parsley. As the minutes ticked by the sauce deepened in color and aroma, becoming a luscious, earthy red. With satisfaction, I leaned back and breathed in the intoxicating scent that was the result of my hard work and dedication. The anticipation of sharing the meal with Tessa filled me with warmth and joy, which would make the end result all that much more fulfilling.

As the sun went down and the sounds of Tessa stirring came from my small room, the water began to boil. By the time Tessa came out of my room, dressed in only one of my shirts, I had set a candlelit table with two plates filled with food and two glasses of red wine. I had put the rest of the meal into the fridge for Ash when he woke.

"Is this all for me?" Tessa said with a slight smile.

"Well, I may have got carried away," I laughed and rubbed the back of my head.

"No, it's perfect," she said and kissed the tip of my nose. "Though now I feel underdressed."

"Hmm, I think you're a little overdressed," I purred and kissed her softly.

She batted at me and laughed. "Down boy," she then looked at me seriously, "As much as I love this… I need to go feed. I will be back for that dinner though, so don't go anywhere."

"Should I come with you?" I asked worriedly.

"I… I don't want you to see me like that. There are times I get a little out of control and need to be forced off," winced Tessa.

"I want to know every part of you," I grabbed her hand.

I pulled her against me and put her hand against my heart.

"I will never see you as anything but that shy, beautiful woman I fell in love with," I said and kissed her forehead.

She blushed and pulled away, "In time. Not this time. Once you are safer."

"I don't need protecting," I pouted.

She was gone without another word and I sat at the table and played with the noodles as I waited for her.

Chapter Twenty-Four

I don't know how long I sat there moping, after having worked so hard to make dinner and being alone for it, when the door opened. I hadn't locked it and assumed it was Tessa. I looked up with a smile across my face and saw someone I hadn't seen in a while. James Davis. The newest werewolf to have joined Ash's group, and someone I hadn't seen since my birthday. A lifetime ago that seemed.

"Food? Oh, great, man," said James.

"Ash just fell asleep a few hours ago. He was up all night and today. I'll tell him you came by," I said; my smile fell into a frown.

"Actually, I had come to see him, but I was told by that vampire you two were bonded with to get you to come quick. Something happened and I just happened to be coming up," said James.

"We should wake, Ash," I said, and went to turn around.

"Hey, you got me. I'm sure the three of us can handle whatever has her in a tizzy. Like you said, he is probably exhausted, so he won't be too much help that way," James said and grabbed my shoulder.

He had moved from the door to me faster than I could see. I shrugged. If Tessa was in trouble, then time was important. I followed him out the door, I didn't even bother to lock it as I left. I ran as fast as I could after James, but he outpaced with no effort. I paid no attention to where we were

123

going, my sole focus was on getting to Tessa as quickly as possible. I turned down an alley to follow, and he was gone. There was nothing there. An empty alley was all I faced. I walked down, keeping an eye on the dumpsters that anyone could hide behind as I closed the distance.

"James?" I called out as I got to the end of the alley.

I searched for a secret entrance in the brick wall, but I found nothing in the minutes I spent searching.

"Hello? Anyone?" I called out.

I reached for my phone and realized I had no pockets and no phone. I ran to the alley entrance and tried to find a landmark I could recognize. The buildings were rundown, with boarded-over windows and broken glass. The only light I had was the moonlight; even the streetlamps in this part of town didn't work. I hadn't noticed because of the clear night and the full moon.

Then my mind began to work. James had come into the house on the full moon. Something was very wrong. I needed to find Tessa or get back to Ash. Preferably both. I was an idiot. I walked around absentmindedly when people started to emerge from nearby alleys. They were covered in ratty clothes, but they weren't the usual homeless I was used to. For one, they didn't usually have orange eyes that glowed in the moonlight. Ten of them surrounded me, a sneer on their faces.

"The feast is here," said one.

"How did he survive?"

"Maybe it's a twin?"

"No matter. This time we get to feast."

"The body will not be found by those who search the shadows for us."

"I'm such an idiot. You can't kill me. And I don't want

to die," I mumbled as I backed into a wall.

"Your pain will be so delicious."

I also wasn't sure that I couldn't die. So far, everything I had known was wrong. Werewolves and vampires weren't real, until they were. I could die, until I couldn't. Vampires couldn't taste my blood or smell me, and now these things around me very much could. What if they could kill me for good? A blur of fur flashed by, and I closed my eyes. A cold snout touched my arm, and I jumped. My eyes opened to see eye to eye with a massive wolf with amber eyes that seemed familiar.

"Mrs. Ulfr?" I asked.

The wolf nodded. Around her were a dozen other wolves, snarling and staying away from me. With a howl from Lyra the wolves dispersed, except her. She motioned with her head to follow, and I did. It took a while, but we got back to my apartment before she left me alone again. I ran up the stairs and saw the door had been broken in. The couch was flipped over, the TV was broken, and both bedroom doors had been ripped off their hinges. I ran to Ash's room, and Tessa stood at the edge of the bed. There was blood everywhere.

"What happened? Where's Ash?" I asked from the doorway.

"I... I... This was like this when I returned," said Tessa.

She turned to look at me; she had been crying.

She ran into me with a bear hug, "I thought you had been taken. Is Ash with you?"

I wrapped her tightly in my arms and pressed her against me, "No. I left him here, asleep. I was told you were in trouble."

"Told? By who?"

"One of the people who was from the pack Ash ran with for the longest time. He was the newest member. He said he had come to see Ash, but that he had run into you, and you needed me to come. Then he left me… surrounded by those darker vampires."

"Did… did you die again?" she cried.

"No, I was saved and brought back home. By Mrs. Ulfr, actually."

"It's his blood," Tessa murmured. "All that blood is from Ash."

"But he's alive, right? They wouldn't take his body if he were dead."

"I don't know. But we have to find him."

"Can you track where he was taken?"

She shook her head, "I don't have a sense of smell that good."

"What a great time for Yujin to be weakened," I muttered. We need to find someone who can help us."

"Do you know any of his other friends?"

"No… I couldn't even begin to tell you where to find them. I don't even know where the teacher would be since the semester hasn't started."

I found my phone and called his parents, but, of course, they didn't answer. They were out prowling. They had come a long way, and I hadn't even thought to ask where they would be staying. Morning would be too late. I ran out of the house, and without saying anything, Tessa followed me. I had hoped Lyra was still around, but when Tessa made no mention of anything, I just kept moving toward Isiak's mansion. To my surprise, the door didn't open when I got to it. I tried the handle, and it was locked. I stepped back and looked at it in confusion. Tessa stepped by me, and with a small twist of her shoulder, the door flew open. She stepped to the side to let me go in.

I kissed her cheek, "I knew I kept you around for a reason."

"Least I'm useful for something," she said somberly.

I stopped in the foyer and looked down each direction, "Want to be even more useful and take me to Yujin?"

"If he's here. I don't know if he left or not," Tessa said as she looked down the halls, "And this quiet is weirding me out."

I followed her through the maze-like house and gazed down the halls that we passed, "Where is everyone?"

"I want to go find out," she said, stopping at an intersection. Something is massively wrong."

The path in front of us was blocked off, almost like it had collapsed in, but the roof and walls were still intact.

"That is not normal," I said.

"That end of the hall is also where great-great grandpa would be."

"Can we get through?"

"I can try. I need to find something…" she trailed off as she disappeared.

I looked around and tried to find anything I could try to move out of the collapsed section. Nothing felt like it was small enough or light enough for me to move, as I tested multiple sections.

"Move," Tessa said as I pulled at a beam.

"Yea, ma'am," I said and backed away.

She had a black pole like the ones used by the police to break down doors. She lifted it up with one arm and threw it. It smashed through the debris with little effort and traveled a few more feet down the hall. The hole it made filled up as the debris fell, but there was enough room now we could climb over the top. The cracked door stood there, closed and unbroken, as we got to it. I hesitated at the door, debating on knocking or going in when it opened.

"Is it safe?" Isiak asked as he looked down the hall.

"What happened?" I asked, "Why is the hall blocked off?"

He let us in, and the only people in the room were Rafael, Isiak, and Corri.

"We were attacked," Isiak explained, "They had come to look for Tessa, but she had just left."

"Where is everyone?" Tessa asked with fear in her eyes.

"Master Yujin was out to feed," began Rafael, "But he left me with strict instructions. If something came while he was out, I was to get who I could back into this room and press the button on the back wall."

"Where is everyone else? Jarret? Jeffery? Dolores? A dozen people were here when I left," Tessa said, water welling in her eyes.

"I was not fast enough to alert them. I am not worthy of being used by the Master," said Rafael.

"You didn't see them?" Corri asked.

"There was nobody around," I said as I put an arm around Tessa. "We were hoping to get help."

"We can't help anyone," growled Isiak. "Everything has been taken from us. Our livestock are gone. Our family was brutally murdered. I could hear the sounds of their screams and could do nothing to stop it."

Tessa turned to me and wrapped her arms around me.

"They came for Ash, also. They have to be up to something. There was no blood, no bodies, nothing," I said as I rubbed Tessa's back.

"Whoever did this, I will rip them to shreds," snarled Isiak.

"You'd be just as dead as them," Tessa said coldly as she turned around, her eyes a deep purple. "But now I am angry. They've taken my family and people I care about. They tried to kill the person I love and, as Matriarch of this family, I refuse to become just a victim."

Isiak and Corri knelt, the pressure from Tessa forcing them too. Their eyes turned crimson, and they snarled.

"Rise, we go hunting," Tessa roared.

And just like that, I was standing alone with Rafael.

Chapter Twenty-Five

I stood there, unsure what I could do. I hated feeling so powerless. Even as a scion, I was still left feeling invisible. I was not going to be left behind like I was someone that needed to be protected. I made my way out of the small room and to the first intersection. I needed to find my way out, but all the twists and turns made it hard to keep track of which way to go. A tap on my shoulder caused me to jump. Rafael had followed me and motioned for me to follow him. I lowered my head in embarrassment as I followed the old man out.

"As much as I think you should stay here, I know you won't. That is why the Master took an interest in you," said Rafael.

"Thanks for the help. If he comes back, tell him what happened. Those three won't be enough," I sighed.

I didn't know where to start, so I just picked a direction to walk back towards my apartment. Ash was gone, Tessa was roaming around in a rage, and Yujin was gone. The only solace I had was that my parents had been spared this insanity. I guess there were some things to be said for being completely normal.

At the apartment I looked around for any clues, not that I knew what to really look for. The whole place was a mess. Spaghetti and sauce were all over the place; wine stained the carpets, and the walls were cracked from the force of thrown chairs and the couch. But Ash had been in his

room when they took him, so why had it been ransacked?
The blood had gone from a lot in the room to having tiny
amounts along the way to the front door, there was none
anywhere else. I started to pick up, angry at myself. I couldn't
do anything when there was a knock on the door.

"Yes?" I called out.

"Is Ashlan here?" came Lyra's voice.

I rushed to the door and flung it open.

"Mrs. Ulfr! You've saved me again!" I wrapped her in
a hug.

She pushed me away and glared down at me, "What is
going on? Why is this house a mess? Where is Ashlan?"

"He's gone," I whispered. "When you showed me
back home, I found out he was missing when I came up."

She pushed past me and looked around. She turned
into her wolf form and sniffed around. She turned to go out
the door, and I blocked the closed door.

"I am not being left behind. Ash is MY best friend.
I can help, and I am tired of being ignored when everyone I
care about could be in danger," I said with a raised voice.

She bared her teeth at me, then returned to human
form, "Fine. I'm not really mad at you, anyway. Everything
that has happened isn't your fault. Hang on to me tightly."

She turned back into the massive wolf and leaned
down so that I could get on her back. I grabbed a jacket from
the door and put my phone in a pocket before I climbed on.
I had to close my eyes against the wind once she was down
the stairs and out of the door. She stopped at intervals and
sniffed the air before she took off full sprint again. She
stopped and shook me off after what seemed like hours. I
looked around as I got my legs steady under me. We were
on a darkened street, with houses that were run-down, with

broken doors and tarps that covered windows.

"Why'd we stop?" I asked.

"He's close. But I can't get the exact area. It seems to come from everywhere on this block," Lyra said, her face scrunched up in anger and confusion.

"We need to get help. The things that took Ash are too strong for just us."

She took out her phone and made a quick call to Ulric. I sent a quick text to Tessa to tell her I had found Ash, then shared my location with her.

"If I ever find out who did this, I will rip them to shreds," growled Lyra.

"Cazimir," I said. "At least that's been my guess. Unless Yujin is seriously playing us all."

"Where did you hear that name?"

"It's a long story."

"It's a false story. Cazimir was a great wolf. And he has been dead since the beginning of our people. Killed by a vampire. The start of this war between lycan and vampires."

"What if... it wasn't. What if there was more to it?"

"Our history has been shared orally since the dawn of time. We know what happened."

"Oh, yes. Oral history, never changing as it's spread down the lines for billions of years," I muttered sarcastically.

She slapped me and my head snapped to the side, "I thought we helped raise you better than to be so sarcastic to your elders, Rai Eckles."

She crossed her arms and scowled at me. I rubbed my cheek and looked down.

"Sorry, ma'am."

She embraced me in a hug and let me go when the sound of footsteps came in the distance. Ulric and a dozen other people came up the street. After a quick hug to Ulric, she turned to the rest of the pack.

"Our alpha is somewhere around here. We need to find him," she said.

The group transformed and split into groups of two and moved out, leaving me the lone man out. I looked at my phone and saw no new messages, so I went to the first house. I crept up and looked into one of the broken windows. The meager moonlight didn't penetrate the darkness inside, so I couldn't see anything inside. I shouldered my way into the warped door and used my phone as a flashlight. I scanned the dusty house. Webs were in every corner I could see and the couches were molded. Rats scattered as the light hit them.

"Hello?" I yelled into the darkness.

The only sound was skittering and the groaning of a house settling. I took a step in when I was yanked back by the collar of my shirt. The doorframe where I had been standing exploded outwards, and then I was facing the street. Slender arms were wrapped around me in a protective manner as I stared befuddled at the street.

"You need to stop walking into places alone," Tessa said, her voice a low growl in my ear.

"Sorry," I muttered.

"That creature is taken care of," Isiak said as he walked in front of me from the house.

"What was it?" I asked as I pulled away from Tessa and turned to face the trio.

"Our darker brethren. The kind we normally deal with. Must have been trying to find a place of solitude," Corri said as she cleaned blood off her hands with a handkerchief.

"Could he be in there?" I looked at Tessa, the fear evident in my eyes.

133

"He isn't. They would have more around him. Come with me so I know you're safe," Tessa said, intertwining her fingers with mine.

The feeling of her being so close dropped some of the anger I had felt earlier, and the fear along with it. As long as we were together, we would find Ash. Corri and Isiak led the way.

"This game of cat and mouse is growing old to me," boomed a voice that rattled me to my core, "Follow the lights and come see me. If you dare, my children."

The streetlamps lit up one by one, but only certain ones. The werewolves turned into hybrid form and followed the trail of lights. Corri and Isiak followed, with me and Tessa bringing up the rear. I kept a grip on her hand as we walked. My heart raced in fear and anticipation. Whoever that voice belonged to chilled me to the bone, and that was just from those couple of sentences.

"It'll be okay," Tessa whispered as we walked and leaned over and kissed my cheek. "I won't let anything happen to you or Ash."

"Thanks," I murmured, now worried she'd get herself hurt trying to save Ash or me.

The lights led us to a small, half-collapsed cabin, where a large, muscular man with long, dark red hair that covered his face sat on the steps leading up to the porch. My eyes widened as dozens of people stood around the house, and on the porch itself, tied up and unmoving, was Ash.

"I am so glad you all decided to come," the man flashed a toothy grin up at us, "Even bringing these bats to play."

"Who are you?" Ulric boomed.

"My dear Children of the Moon, do you not

recognize the progenitor of your kind?" mocked the man, and he stood up.

As he stood on the steps, he loomed over everyone. His eyes seemed to glow orange, and as fur grew out of him, his body twisting and distorting into the giant two-legged wolf shape, his canines grew even longer into fine, thin points. The stairway underneath him collapsed under the weight. He was almost as tall as the cabin as he stepped forward. His arms were out to the sides, and his toothy maw was pulled back into a hideous grin.

"I am the only original of our kind left. You ask me who I am, yet you know deep inside the answer to that question," he said as he strode into the crowd of werewolves, "Now say my name."

"Cazimir," said a cacophony of werewolves as they knelt.

Of the wolves, only the Ulfr's stayed standing.

"Why do you not kneel before your God?" Cazimir asked as he stood over the couple.

"There's only one God. Whatever you may be, you are not it," said Ulric. "You also took my son. I'd just as soon you release him so we can go more than anything else."

"If that is your child, then I did you a favor. He was consorting with the likes of a demigod and a vampire. You can make better children, ones who won't be such disappointments in the future," scoffed Cazimir.

Cazimir rocked back as Ulfric lashed out with an uppercut to his face. Cazimir caught the next punch in an enormous palm.

"I see. You have a misguided love for the heathen," said Cazimir, as the disgust dripped from his voice.

"You're one to talk big, dark, and ugly," I called out.

"You're part vampire."

His head snapped towards me, a snarl on his face, "I am something better than that."

"Oh yeah? You're hanging out with those things," I said as I walked towards him and pointed to the vampires surrounding us.

Tessa touched my shoulder, but I shrugged her off and stood next to Cazimir.

"These things are merely tools I use. I do not sympathize with these… failures," Cazimir said.

"Well, Mr. God, last I checked, you haven't sent any werewolves after me," I puffed out my chest.

"You have been a hard one to kill. I don't know how you've stayed alive. Incompetent tools, I see. I was assured you had been slain on the beach that day," Cazimir said as he rubbed the bridge of his nose. "Your kind started this whole mess."

"Did they?" boomed a familiar voice.

Yujin appeared next to me and caused me to jump away.

"Great-great grandfather!" exclaimed Tessa.

"You have finally shown your face after all these years," laughed Cazimir. "I have not seen you since I sent you running off into the night."

"Maybe I needed a reminder that I could no longer run," Yujin said and looked down at me.

"Let my friend go," I said as I stood as tall as I could next to Yujin.

"Do you know how these abominations are created? Vampires. They are not killed when they are turned. They have the air of death around them and become walking undead with the turning. But these creatures I made so long ago, with the help of Yujin's brothers, were made from death itself. Their deaths were the catalyst for me to figure out the transformative abilities of what happens when you kill someone you turn. It took… a while to make a hybrid. So many of my kind died until I found the right sequence to make it happen. One of the original survivors was crafty enough to survive and get away, whereas I killed every other hybrid I was able to make. I assumed it was a failure. Born of my own genetic template, I had such hope before I left it to die in the heap. But, to my surprise, it did not," Cazimir said with a laugh, "The end of that line lies on that porch."

"So, it does seem I was wrong in some aspects," Yujin said as he stroked his chin.

"Ash is related to you?" I was horrified.

"As is this man who punched me. My fire goes deep inside him also," Cazimir grinned.

"I don't care what you are. Who you are. I am taking my son and leaving," Ulric said, oddly cool.

His eyes raged with fire that his voice didn't have. Besides him, Lyra had that same fire raging in her eyes. The rest of the werewolves looked back between the couple and Cazimir.

"I think it is time to end my line. Rise my wolves!" bellowed out Cazimir.

The other werewolves obediently stood up and bared their teeth at the Ulfr's as they transformed into their massive wolf forms.

"Stop this right now!" bellowed Yujin.

"You have no power here," Cazimir said as he stalked over to Yujin. "You are just an old washed-up relic."

"Maybe. But your targets are gone now," grinned Yujin.

137

Cazimir and I looked around to see the vampires I had come with were gone, and so were the Ulfr's. Cazimir roared in anger and grabbed Yujin around the body. His hand in the giant hybrid form almost wrapped around Yujin's small body and pinned his arms down.

"My kind are still good at running from you," cackled Yujin, "I guess this is my own ending."

"What about Ash?" I asked.

"My little Tessa has him, I am sure," sighed Yujin. "Do run yourself. I don't want the last memory of me to be my death."

I hit Cazimir in the thigh as hard as I could and hurt my own hand more than I affected him. He looked down at me with a brow raised. Yujin laughed out loud.

"I'm not leaving him alone. So come on, fight me ugly," I said and put up my fists.

Cazimir rolled his eyes at me and turned back to Yujin as he lifted him up.

"Now, my old rival, this rivalry shall end," Cazimir said, opening his mouth wide.

"Break out, Yujin! Come on!" I yelled.

He waved to me, and I saw that his hand was still blackened. I fell to my knees. As Cazimir's mouth came down on Yujin's head, I was left with the knowledge that Yujin had been bluffing the whole time. He had not regenerated fully after I had burned him. Yujin's lifeless body fell next to me as I heard the sound of bones crunching, Cazimir chewing on the whole head of Yujin.

"Now, where were we, little wannabe god?" Cazimir said as he turned to me.

I looked up at the blood-covered muzzle and didn't know what to feel. Yujin had done nothing but use me. He had toyed with my life, and I couldn't really say that his death hit me in a sad way. But without him, because of something I did, this monster would end the lives of everyone. Yujin was better than this thing in front of me, which acted like it was above humanity or Tessa. He stood over me; blood dripped from his fur and dotted my legs as I glared at him.

"Your savior is dead. The one I hunted for so long is no more. Now I will kill you, then find those other six that ran off and kill them. It's a long road, but now I can finally become the ruler of creation like I was meant to be," howled Cazimir.

"No," I growled.

He poked me in the chest with a large claw, "You will taste so sweet to me. I am glad my tools never got to kill you. It's been a while since I have tasted the blood and flesh of a demigod."

I scowled at him with the fire burning inside of me that I was still not used to feeling. My heart felt like it was on fire, and I doubled over and held my chest.

"Don't cry. This world shall fall into the darkness it deserves. I am the only God the ones I allow to survive will know," Cazimir said, not understanding my gasps of pain.

He grabbed me the same way he had Yujin and pinned my hands against my chest. I howled out in pain as the fire spread through my veins and my bones cracked. I fought down the fire inside as it built up. It threatened to explode, and I wanted it to build as much as possible as Cazimir cackled at my pain. My arms were the first bones I felt break, followed by the ribs. The pain was too much for me to bear, and I felt my world growing very dim. I struggled to keep conscious. I wasn't sure if the power would fade away or explode out, and I wanted to be sure the latter happened.

Cazimir brought me towards his widened maw, and I almost did not realize what was happening. My thoughts were clouded by everything going on inside me.

"Not... dying... so... easy," I groaned out and released the fire I had been holding inside as a sharp ripping feeling touched my neck.

Chapter Twenty-Six

I woke up naked in the arms of Tessa on the street. Ash looked down on me with a sigh of relief on his face. He had an arm on Tessa's back and rubbed it.

"I gotta stop seeing you two like this," I croaked.

"I don't know, I could get used to seeing you like this," joked Ash as his eyes wandered down my body.

"My eyes are up here," I smiled as I stood up.

Tessa slapped me in the shoulder and scowled at me.

"Ow. What was that for?" I cried out.

"Stop scaring me! You were supposed to run too," she said with crossed arms.

"Let's get him some clothes before we kill him for scaring us," Ash laughed.

He put an arm around her, and she sighed before her features softened at me.

"You are right, and he is better this way, though. Do we need to find him anything?" she said.

"Guys... I can't walk home naked. Also, what happened to everything around? The werewolves?" I asked as I looked around.

There was nothing but ashes that had blown into the air from the breeze.

"We were going to ask you," Ash said as he walked away.

There was a duffle bag I hadn't noticed. Inside was a change of clothes that I quickly put on. When I was clothed,

141

Ash picked me up in a bear hug. The clothes were cold against my skin in the cool air of the night after burning alive.

"I thought you were dead for good. Heck for a moment I thought I was dead without getting to see that face again," he said as he crushed me against him.

"I've already been crushed to death once today; please don't do it again," I muttered.

He released me but cupped my chin with his hand firmly. I shivered in the cool air.

"I missed you too, love. I wasn't going to let you die without me around," I said and smiled at him.

The kiss was soft, but my body yearned for more as he pulled away.

"Just don't go doing anything stupid again," he said and released my chin.

"Hmm, did you say something?" I said dreamily.

He shook his head and backed away.

"What happened with great-great grandfather and Cazimir?" Tessa asked, her eyes full of hope.

As I looked, I realized that I hadn't seen Yujin's body either. I didn't know what to say. Tessa looked at me expectantly.

"Yujin was still weakened. He should not have been here at all. He was killed by Cazimir. I think I turned… the body, Cazimir, and the pack, and the other vampires into this ash that is in the air," I said quickly.

She turned away and I wrapped my arms around her from behind. Her fingers intertwined with mine on her stomach, and I kissed her neck softly.

"I'm sorry," I murmured.

"It's fine," she whispered.

Ash wrapped his arms around her from the front,

and we stood there for a moment, entangled in each other on the dark, empty street. Ash kissed the top of her head as we parted.

"We should get back. They might bring an army looking for us, knowing my mother," Ash said.

"How did they even get into the house to grab you?" I asked, "They should never have been."

"It wasn't vampires… I was taken by wolves," Ash said as he looked away.

"James?"

"He was one of them. I woke up when he stabbed a clawed hand through me," said Ash.

I looked at him. He looked like he had the last time I had seen him; not like he was nearly killed. The amount of blood he would have lost would have been immense.

"How do you look so good?" I asked, perplexed.

"Bro, I always look good," Ash smiled, and his dimples caused me to lose my train of thought.

"They're right," said Tessa, "All the blood I saw… You should not be walking around so easily. What happened?"

"Maybe it wasn't my blood," shrugged Ash.

"It was most certainly your blood," said Tessa.

"I don't know what you want me to tell you," Ash said, "It is what it is."

Tessa and I looked at each other, but let it drop momentarily as we walked back to Isiak's house. Lyra grabbed me in a motherly hug when we walked into the main foyer.

"You're safe. I was so worried about you," she cried.

"Thanks. Just don't tell my parents about any of this," I joked.

Ulfric rubbed my head, "You did good standing up to

143

him. Guess you aren't just a weak human after all."

"Thanks. I think."

Lyra slapped him on the arm, "Be nice."

He let out a belly laugh.

"Yujin?" Isiak asked.

"He's gone. Looks like I am fully in charge now," Tessa said as a sadness filled her voice.

"Master," bowed Rafael.

"No. You can be free now," said Tessa.

"I could have gone free anytime I wanted. What waits for an old man like me out in this world? Nothing much that I can tell. I was treated well by Master Yujin, and I know you will treat me well, Master Wentzel," said Rafael, still bowed.

"We can't stay at our apartment," I said, "But I don't know how we can find anything else."

Tessa's eyes lit up and turned to Isiak, "Give this house to Rai."

"Why would I do such a thing? I don't want wet dogs in my house," said Isiak.

"Cause I ordered it. Besides, we can bring in some family, and if Rai owns it and lives here, then our dark brethren cannot get in. The small portion killed out there is not all of them. We will have Ash here, you and Corri, me. Nothing will be able to run us out of here again if we turn this into our fortress against the dark. We have a bonding over the pack and the clan, and we have plenty of room."

"I am not living with my parents," groaned Ash.

'WE are not staying," said Ulric, as Lyra seemed to consider it.

I outwardly sighed in relief.

"In fact, we should be going now. I have to go to work tomorrow," said Ulric.

"I could stay," said Lyra, "Make sure everything is settled."

"No!" Tessa, Ash, and I exclaimed.

"Fine, fine, I know when I'm not wanted," Lyra laughed.

She took her husband's hand, and they went off into the night.

"I guess I will need to get the deed. It will take a few days. I am sure you three can survive that long," Isiak said coldly.

"Well, we've survived this night. I think we can survive a few more days. We need to clean up the place anyway," I said.

Chapter Twenty-Seven

It took Isiak longer, conveniently, to get the deed than he said. But it was still only about a week later as we had filled a moving van with the last of our stuff. The van had just left with the movers, bought by Tessa's sudden influx of money from Yujin, and I found Ash as he stood at the edge of the bed that used to be his. The rooms in the mansion had, again, thanks to Tessa, a much bigger bed for us to share.

"This is the last time I will see this room," Ash said. "So many memories in this place."

"A lot of good ones," I said and walked up next to him. "We worked all night on many projects in here."

"But some things I do regret," Ash said and turned to me, "The last time we were in here together, I admit I was jealous of Tessa. I said some things cause I felt territorial of you. But I still had feelings about you outside of that."

"Well, you can make that up to me. And we can leave this room with a pleasant memory," I grinned and reached out to touch his torso.

He felt different... like ice. The usual warmth of his body was not reaching through his shirt. I pulled my hand back and looked up at him.

"No heartbeat either," sighed Ash.

I ran my hand under his shirt and stopped my hand over his heart. He went to pull away, but I just moved closer.

"It's fine. That's why you avoided touching me after that night, why you stayed here away from Tessa, and why

146

you've healed so easily," I said.

He looked away.

"Ashlan, I love you no matter what. You are still you," I ran my hand down his torso and tugged at the top of his pants, "WE can still make this room have one more good, pleasurable memory."

As he took off his shirt, I ran my hand over his thigh and felt the hardness. I smirked at him and grabbed it. He jumped at the suddenness of it but then grinned at me. I pushed him back onto the bed and undid his belt as I kissed his cold torso. I slid off his pants and boxers and stared at his naked, aroused form in awe. He was perfect. My eyes hungrily took in the one thing I wanted; my body yearned for him. I saw the same hunger in his eyes, and I slowly stripped out of my clothes as I watched him get harder. I crawled on top of him and took him in my hand. I kissed his neck as he moaned softly, which made my body ache more for him. I moved my hand slowly as I kissed him on the lips. He returned it with a fierce hunger as his hands explored my body. I bit his lip as his hand roamed my thigh. When it found what it was looking for, I gasped in pleasure and my hand worked faster. As he neared climax, I stopped my strokes and moved my hand up his body as he whimpered.

"Not so fast," I cooed into his ear.

"Who am I to disobey?" he smiled.

I moaned louder than I had meant to as his hand continued its play. His smile made me moan even louder as I grabbed him, and I felt it get even harder as I did. He flipped me over, and our tongues intertwined as his hands made me feel things I had never experienced. My nails dug into his back, and my breathing came short and quick, and he kissed my neck. Each sensual little kiss was electrifying, and I clawed his back as he stopped right before my own climax.

"Not fair," I pouted.

"Now you know how I feel," his smile alone was almost enough to push me over the brink.

He kissed my neck again as his hands explored my body, and my fingers curled into his short hair. After I couldn't take the teasing any longer, I forced his hand where I wanted it to go, and he sucked on my neck as I groaned in pleasure. My hand found its way to where he wanted it, and I could hear his grunts of pleasure as he stayed at my neck. My hand moved faster with urgency as I grew closer to my own completion. I moaned as my pleasure reached its max, simultaneously with Ash's. That was when I felt the fangs pierce my neck. I pushed him away, and the blood ran down his lips as his eyes were an orange color. Those eyes were filled with fear and sorrow as he looked down at me, covered in blood and other things. He jumped back to his feet, and his eyes turned back to their normal ocean blue.

"I'm so sorry, I don't know what ha..." he started.

He doubled over in pain as he howled out. I sat up and scooted back against the wall. I was waiting for the dream to end, but I knew it wasn't going to. This was real. The pain in the side of my neck told me as much. I didn't know what to do. My best friend for my entire existence was about to die, and it was because of me. I sat frozen in fear as he started to glow a bright white. I had to close my eyes. The heat and the light felt like I was close to the sun. His screams of agony tore at my very soul.

Chapter Twenty-Eight

The scream died before the light did. My friend was burned to ashes, and I kept my eyes closed because I did not want to see that. There were some things I could take, some losses that were acceptable, but not him. Anyone but him would have been fine at that moment. I jumped as a large hand ruffled my hair. I opened my eyes, saw that familiar dimpled smile, and gasped.

"I can see ghosts now?" I whimpered.

"I'm not a ghost," laughed Ash heartily.

"Then what happened?"

He just shrugged and sat next to me, "But whatever it is, we need to get you cleaned up. I could lick you clean," he added suggestively.

I jumped on him in a hug, "I can't believe you survived! You big oaf, you scared me."

"Scared myself. And now I need a shower also. I really don't know what happened, but that's for another time. Let's get a shower. I'll wash you and you can wash me."

"Deal," I smiled and kissed him.

Our tongues danced with each other for a moment before we pulled back. The shower was anything but quick; in fact, the hot water ran out before we decided to get out. I watched him get dressed and took in every facet of his body. I had almost lost him, and something had saved him. When we finished dressing, I gave him another giant hug, which he returned.

"Let's not tell, Tessa, about my almost death. I think we've both died enough for one week," Ash said as we walked out of the apartment.

I nodded my agreement and took his hand in mine, which he kissed. We set out on a slow walk, hand in hand, to our new place where the dreamiest wife waited for us. When we got there, she was still asleep, but the sun was getting lower in the sky, and she would be up within the next hour. We started moving things into the places that we wanted them. I was excited to try the kitchen for the first time. My plans for dinner were already set, but there was still plenty of time to start the homemade pizza. We had plans for a movie in the theater room that Ash had picked out. So, I had no idea what we were in for with that. Then Tessa picked the dessert. Which, if I knew her, were going to be milkshakes.

I got lost in setting up a shelf, and I jumped and hit my thumb with a hammer as I felt a small cold hand touch my shoulder. I looked up as I sucked my thumb to see Tessa laugh at me.

"Not funny," I mumbled with my finger still in my mouth.

"Kinda is," she said, pulling my thumb to her lips.

She kissed it and let my hand fall.

"How was the big bed?" I asked.

"Well, it was kinda cold. Nobody was there to hold me," she smiled at me.

"I'm going to freeze next to both of you. Who is going to warm me?" I joked.

"What do you mean?" she asked with a raised brow.

"Oh… Ash. He's like Cazimir now. That's why he healed so quickly. He's a hybrid," I said and looked down now that I had spoiled the secret.

"Impossible... Is that why he's been so distant?"

"Yea. But I got him over that. I think he might have wanted to tell you himself, though."

"Where is he?"

"Uhm... last I saw, he was sunbathing. He grew bored of putting things up," I laughed.

"Well, let's go find the good boy," she said, pulling me to my feet.

I kissed her on the nose and grinned. She smiled, kissed me softly, and walked away. When we found Ash, he was in the middle of a nap in the backyard with his shirt over his face. Tessa licked her lips and leaned against me.

"Think we can just have him right now before dinner?" she purred lustfully.

"There will be plenty of time for that," I laughed and pushed her away.

"Fine," she sighed and rolled her eyes.

As she walked forward, she stopped and sniffed the air. She looked at me, then back to Ash.

"I thought you said he was changed?" she asked, confused.

"Yea. He had no heartbeat. He was also freezing."

"What are you guys talking about?" Ash groaned groggily.

"Rai said that you're a hybrid now," Tessa said as she moved next to Ash.

"Yea. I guess I was meant to become Cazimir's second in command or something," Ash said as he took the shirt off his head.

"Do you not feel the hunger?" asked Tessa.

"Actually, I don't right now. Like I did earlier today, but after I bit..." trailed off Ash.

151

"Bit who?" asked Tessa.

I rubbed the back of my head and looked down as Ash glanced my way.

"You did what?" exclaimed Tessa, "How are either of you alive?"

"Well… in my defense, I can't die," I muttered, "Though that old age thing might catch up to me."

"I… couldn't control myself. I was lost in the moment, and the hunger just surged through me," Ash said shamefully, "I don't know how I survived. I should be dead instead of undead."

"That's the thing. You aren't part vampire," she said.

"I think I know what I am," Ash said harshly.

Tessa grabbed my hand and pushed it against Ash's chest. My eyes grew wide.

"What's with that look?" asked Ash.

"You… have a heartbeat. And you're warm," I stuttered.

"Impossible," Ash said, moving my hand away to feel it.

"What happened?" Tessa asked.

"I don't really know. I just felt an intense pain, and then I was fine," said Ash.

"He glowed with an intense light and gave off immense heat. I couldn't even look at what happened because it was too bright," I said.

"Ra, the sun god, who is reborn with the light of the sun. Your blood is like the sun to us. A cleansing light that washes away everything," Isiak called down from a balcony.

"What does that even mean?" I asked as I looked up at him.

Isiak shrugged and walked inside without an answer.

"It doesn't matter," said Tessa.

She smacked Ash on the arm.

"And you, don't do anything stupid like that again. Especially without talking to me first," she scolded.

"Fine, I won't do anything stupid until I tell you I'm going to do it," Ash said with an eye roll.

"Is he still a werewolf?" I asked expectantly.

"Yes," Tessa said as Ash went wolf form.

"I don't understand anything," I said with a sigh.

"Neither do we," Ash said.

"Well, I might..." said Tessa.

"How?" Ash and I said simultaneously.

"Follow me," Tessa said.

We followed Tessa to the large library. The one thing I was excited to explore once everything was settled. She walked with a purpose and stopped at a small section of ancient-looking tomes.

"The answer will definitely be here," she said, scanning the titles.

"How can you read those titles?" I asked.

"I taught myself how to read hieroglyphics. I had nothing else to do with my time. I learned a lot of languages since this library is so extensive," Tessa said nonchalantly.

Me and Ash looked at each other. I had tried to learn Spanish in high school, but it hadn't stuck with me. And Ash basically did the least amount of learning he could to make his parents happy. It was the only reason he even went to college and not just tried to become a pro surfer.

"Here it is," Tessa said and pulled out a book.

On the cover, a falcon-headed man sat down with a crook and flail in crossed hands. An orange ball was over his head. A woman looked to be serving him something.

"What is that?" I asked.

"Egyptian gods," said Tessa.

I lifted an eyebrow.

"There are a lot of gods. Few have any association with Phoenix, though. Ra is one of those. And he is reborn every morning. The sun would go down, and Ra would go to the underworld. He would battle Apophis and the dark minions. The fact the sun came up means that Ra and his warriors won, and Ra would be reborn for the day," explained Tessa, "I think what Isiak was telling us is that you are the child of Ra."

"I'm the child of an Egyptian sun god? No shot. I'm not even Egyptian," I protested.

"I don't think that really matters. Whatever these ancient gods are, they exist, but there were some before Egypt, Greece, Scandinavia, and every other race that existed. If they are all from the time of great-great-grandfather and Cazimir, then Ra wouldn't be Egyptian either," Tessa said.

"But who was my mother?"

"I'm not sure it matters," said Tessa.

"It does to me. Like why was I given up? Is that just something I will never know?"

"It happens. You have two parents that love you, though," said Tessa.

"She is right. Don't worry about it. So you're Rai, child of Ra. Doesn't change anything," added Ash.

"I mean, we can do a DNA test and see if anything turns up. But don't get too excited just in case it doesn't," said Tessa.

"Let's do that. Maybe she knows something," I said.

"Wouldn't bet on it," said Tessa.

Ash nudged her with his shoulder, "I'm sure it'll work

out, my dude."

"Yes, everything will go smoothly. That is the life we live," I said sarcastically.

The night went by in a blur for me. The pizza I made was done less with the love I usually have for making food, and more with automation. I don't remember the movie we watched or anything, really. Tessa laid with me and Ash as we went to sleep, but if she stayed long, I couldn't even tell you. That morning, I found Rafael and set about getting a DNA test done. The next two months, I could think of nothing else. School had started again, and I was barely passing any classes, as I couldn't concentrate as I waited for the results. I might not find a mother or father, but maybe someone that could lead me to the one who gave birth to me.

After classes, I got home, and Rafael handed me a manila envelope. I wanted to rip it open, but at the same time, I was scared. Ash wasn't home yet, and Tessa was still asleep, so I put it on the dresser in our room and proceeded to stare at it from the edge of the bed where Tessa slept.

I don't know how long I was there. It had to have been hours, because Ash was out of class, and he came to the room to change and saw me sitting there. He changed, and I didn't even take my eyes off the envelope.

"Are you okay?" Ash asked as he shook me back to reality.

"What. No. I mean, yes. I mean, I don't know. The envelope from the DNA test came back," I murmured.

"What did it say?" Ash asked.

"I haven't looked at it at all. I'm too scared."

"I'll do it."

"No!" I cried out as he reached for it.

"Why not?"

"There is too much in there. So many new things I can learn. I want to open it. I just… I'm scared."

He kissed the top of my head, "I'm here with you. We can wait until Tessa is up, and we can all be together when you open it."

"How long is that?"

He looked at his phone, "A half hour, give or take."

"I'll start dinner. Then afterwards…" I said, then left the room.

I chose two prime cuts of beef tenderloin from the fridge and set the oven to heat up to Four Hundred and Twenty-Five. I seasoned the beef with a gratuitous amount of salt and pepper before I coated them with a layer of Dijon mustard to add a hint of tang to complement the savory flavors. As the beef marinated, I started to chop various mushrooms. Once I was done with that, I sauteed them with shallots, garlic, and a bit of red wine until they formed an earthy paste that would serve as the bed for the beef. When I was done, I pulled out two sheets of puff pastry that would encase the beef. I then spread a thin layer of prosciutto ham over the pastry before I spread the mushroom duxelles over that. The flavors, together with the beef, would be perfect when it was fully cooked.

I wrapped the beef with all of it and sealed it up. With a brush of beaten egg, I gave the pastry a golden hue that would make the exterior the crispiness and flakiness that every good beef wellington needed. As I put it into the oven, Tessa floated into the kitchen with a good morning kiss.

"You are planning on serving shakes with this too, right?" she asked sleepily after the kiss.

"Whatever you want, my dear," I said with a half-smile.

As it cooked, we watched a show. Tessa lay curled up with her head in my lap as I leaned against Ash, who wrapped his arm around me. I knew vampires didn't need to eat, but something inside me was still saddened every time Isiak and Corri turned down my invite for dinner. But once the beef wellington was done, I made sure Rafael sat with us. I was not going to let him miss out on perfection.

I also used it as a reason to push back the time before I opened that manila envelope that scared me. It was also why I chose beef wellington to make. It took a while. Convincing Rafael to eat with us took almost as long. I even offered to make ice cream from scratch for milkshakes, but Ash shot me down and sent Rafael to get some from the diner I hadn't been to in what seemed like forever.

"You cannot run from this all night," Ash said as he held up the envelope.

"I can try," I muttered.

"Why don't you want to see what's in it?" asked Tessa.

"It's not that. I want to see what is in it. But what if we learn something bad? What if I'm related to like, Charles Manson?" I said.

"What if you are? You were raised by Marcus and Vanessa Eckles. That's all that matters at the end of the day," said Ash.

Tessa put a hand on my shoulder, "And we are here for you. So, let's get this open."

I sat on the couch and opened the envelope slowly. There was a single piece of paper in it. I pulled it out and looked at it blankly.

"What does it say?" asked Ash.

"That they don't appreciate being sent fake DNA. That there is no way the sample we sent could be anything but a prank. That it has none of the markers needed to be real," I said.

Tessa snatched the paper out my hand and read it over. She crumpled it up and threw it against the wall where it fell to the ground.

"This makes no sense. What are they trying to pull?" Tessa seethed.

"I'm not even human at all. Then what am I? Child of Ra, but what else? And why was I left at a church?" I asked.

"I'm sure it was just a glitch in their systems. If we send something else back or to a different place, then maybe we can find something," said Ash.

Rafael walked in as if on cue, holding up several papers.

"Master Yujin had already tried to find out who you were. He sent hair follicles, fingernail clippings, skin, saliva, all of it. He got back all the same results," said Rafael.

I snatched the papers and read through them fast. They all said the same thing.

"I guess great-great grandfather never told you everything, Rafael," Isiak said as he appeared behind me.

I jumped but turned around slowly.

"What do you mean?" asked Tessa.

He held up a letter and handed it to me, "I was told to give this to the scion if he ever tried to find who he was."

It was addressed to me in a scrawled handwriting.

Chapter Twenty-Nine

I opened the letter and read through it.

Dear Scion,
If you are reading this,
you have searched for your parentage.
It took me longer than it should have
for me to find it out.
I am dying tonight by my old nemesis Cazimir,
so I write this letter.
You are a Scion, but you are not a demigod.
You are so much more.
Your parents are not even human.
Ra would be your father.
He was easy to tell.
What wasn't easy to tell is that
two sun gods were the parentage.
Aurora, goddess of the dawn
- that is your mother.

I stared at the words on the paper for what felt like an eternity.

159

"What does it say?" asked Ash expectantly.

"That Ra and Aurora are my parents," I said.

"Who?" asked Ash.

"Aurora? The dawn goddess? Wait... is she a different person than Eos? Did the Romans and Greeks really worship different yet similar gods?" Tessa went off on a tangent.

I didn't hear what else she said. I was not human. That was what set me apart. It was what made it so I couldn't die. I was told that being a scion would make me nothing but a normal human. Not being able to die and being able to explode in fire, It all made sense now. Now I just had to wait for answers to other questions. Would I still age and die? Was I destined to watch Ash die?

I didn't know the answer to those questions back then, and I still don't know now. Only time will tell. Who knows, maybe one day I will even meet these gods that created me and ask them why I was left here.

The End

 Olyn Moon, a Texan writer with a flair for storytelling, heavily influenced by the vibrant world of Japanese animation. Just like anime, Olyn loves to mix it up, dabbling in various genres from fantasy to sci-fi and everything in between. When not lost in the realms of writing, you'll likely find Olyn lost in the world of Tabletop RPG's or deep in the fantasy worlds of video games.